The Grail
of the
Unicorn Planet

An Archie Dixon novel

Vivien Carmichael

Strategic Book Group

Strategic Book Group
P.O. Box 333
Durham CT 06422
www.StrategicBookClub.com

ISBN: 978-1-60976-803-4

This book is dedicated to my two sons, Nick and James, my father Alexander and my husband Denis. It is dedicated also to Caroline, Alice, Archie, Grace, Harry, Stan, Zonah, Chay, Mathew, Harry and Robbie.

About the author

Vivien Carmichael is the only daughter of Scottish parents. She was born and brought up in Brighton. She went to Varndean Grammar School for Girls and undertook a Teacher's Training Course at Manresa House, Roehampton, a branch of Battersea Teachers Training College. She spent a year living in Paris and then returned to London where she met and married her husband. She has two sons, Nick and James and spent some years bringing them up.

Vivien decided to attend Brighton University as a mature student when her youngest son went to school. She successfully gained a BA (Hons) degree in Library and Information Studies. Vivien worked for some years in libraries in London and is now teaching English to foreign students in Brighton.

The Grail of the Unicorn Planet is the second book in the Archie Dixon series. The First book in the series, The Skimming Stone, was first published in 2003 by Nightingale books a branch of Pegasus Publications. ISBN 1 903491 18 5 is now available from Lulu.com.

Acknowledgements

I should like to thank everyone who helped me write this book, and in particular my second husband Denis, a professional market researcher for all his help and encouragement and especially for all the time and energy he spent researching various subjects on the Internet. The Internet is a wonderful tool for research but it does require dedication and time.

Special thanks also to my friend Trake for all the information that she supplied on antibiotics.

My thanks also to Brighton and Hove City Council for their tour of Brighton's sewers, and to Southern Water for all the useful details they provided on Brighton outflow.

And lastly thanks to Rilla at First Editing for her help in putting my book together.

Contents

LIST OF CHARACTERS

Earth characters

Archie	A twelve year old boy and novice wizard.
Ally	His sister, ten years old also a novice wizard.
Zonah	Their friend, a girl ten years old.
Chey	Zonah's younger brother.
Trake	Zonah's mother, a pharmacist.
Jazz	A neighbour of Ally and Archie. An ex WW2 spitfire pilot
Mr M	The mastermind behind the Bank heist.
Paul Denby	Mr M's go between and organiser.
John Hallorhan	An American and ex-Vietnam tunnel rat, recruited by Paul to carry out the tunnelling and bank robbery.
Mr Morgan	The Bank Manager.
Betty	The girls' saviour.
Bert	Betty's husband.
Roa and Mia	Betty's nieces.
Artemis and Adonis	Bert and Betty's twins.
Rufus	A fox, and friend of Signet's
Clytemnestra	Known as Nessie, the head of the parakeet's who live in Hollingdean woods.
Charlie	Ally and Archie's cat

The Immortals

Signet	**A good wizard who protects the Oosha and a friend of Archie and Ally.**
Vastator	**An evil entity who only comes to life when he is called back to Earth by great evil**

Altarian Peoples

<u>**The Elementals**</u>	**Keepers of peace and harmony. Immortals**
• **Kiera**	**Air Diva**
• **Imrir**	**Fire Diva**
• **Assir**	**Water Diva**
• **Erda**	**Earth Diva**

<u>**Unicorns**</u>

• **Asphodel**	**Present ruler of Altair**
• **Aloric**	**Her son, 13 years old**
• **Ambrine**	**Her daughter 12 years old**

<u>**Bean Tighe**</u>

• **Professor Beshley**	**Head of Department of Contagious Diseases Ministry of Medicine**

<u>**Bokwus**</u>

• **Doctor Hokusain**	**Head of Department of Epidemiology, Ministry of Medicine**

<u>Earth Dragons</u>	Keepers of Peace and Harmony on Altair
• Yang Rong	Joint Head of the Department of Peace and Harmony with Yin Zheng
<u>Elves</u>	Shoemakers Owners of tanneries Workers in leather industries.
• Gretorix	Chief of the Elven tribe
• Thorin	Owner of one of the largest tanneries on Altair
• Zelana	Thorin's wife
• Zegar	Thorin's son
• Julian	Thorin's nephew
• Saskaret	Thorin's secretary
• Hott	The foreman of the tannery
• Shokar	One of the tannery workforce
<u>Fenghuang</u>	Keepers of Peace and Harmony on Altair
• YinZheng	Joint Head of the Department of Peace and Harmony with Yang Rong
<u>Flower Fairies</u>	The Bee keepers
• Xandria	an eight year old fairy
• Melix	her younger sister
<u>Gillyaids</u>	
• Colonel Gurin	Gillyaid Security Officer
<u>Kitsune</u>	Law keepers on Altair
• Souhei	A law practitioner

<u>Mizakeen</u>   Have the ability to change their shape

- **Lev**   Co-owner of "The Schlock Shop"
- **Soli**   Co-owner of "The Schlock Shop"

<u>Sylphs</u>

- **Professor Santha**   In charge of Terra Seraim

<u>Shamenites</u>

- **Jocasta**
- **Amadou**   Her son

<u>Tokolyush</u>

- **Doctor Kiddush**   Head of Department of Virology, Ministry of Medicine.

Altairian Animals

- **Grilk**   Omnivorous small rodent, which eats the bark of the Tarran tree as well as insects, grain and smaller creatures.
- **Moratim**   Large bird like turkeys that live on the plains in the Northern territories.
- **Wokbatt**   Large Ox like creatures who are very strong

Prologue

The Quickening

Vastator stirred. He dimly became aware of his own consciousness. From the cold blackness of his hibernation, he became gradually aware of redness and warmth. The ichor began to move sluggishly through his veins. His memories started to return. He was coming to life again. He had made this journey thousands of times from icy blackness to life and back again. But this time things were different. Something about this latest incarnation told him that things would be different.

He was yanked back into existence by the vibrations of manmade evil, which also fed him and kept him alive, as far as he could remember. Now, only good or the absence of evil could send him back to the icy black abyss. Not that Vastator particularly cared what brought him to life or kept him there, just as long as he was alive.

Memories of his most recent life flooded back, a jumble of children, wizards, petty crooks and the stone. Above all, the stone! Vastator had powers he had picked up from his many past lives, from the magi, from the alchemists and from various witches and wizards. But the stone he had come across in his latest life had the most powerful vibrations yet encountered. It was almost certainly the Philosopher's Stone that those crazy alchemists had always sought but had never found.

For Vastator, the stone—or the skimming stone as those

children had called it—had incredible powers and maybe, just maybe, enough power to put an end to his miserable cycle of all too few brief periods of life in an endless ocean of inky, cold blackness. Whatever else he did now in his new life, he had to find that stone again, because with it he could possibly remain forever in the light of life.

Humans meant little to him other than their capacity to bring him back from the stygian darkness he detested. However, in one respect they had qualities that he admired: a determination that sometimes drove their miserable short lives and, in some cases, an aim that even lived beyond them. He remembered the alchemists driven by their quest for the Philosopher's stone, where the next generation of alchemists picked up the baton of the previous generation's efforts. Similarly, he recalled other strange bands of dedicated humans, who sought with a superhuman determination the Holy Grail. The human, as an individual, was nothing. But the determination of their particular quests gave the timeless Vastator a quality to admire. To him, the quest for the stone and the quest for the Holy Grail were one and the same. In that, Vastator could recognise and respect his one and only human quality.

Chapter One

The Sanctuary

After the bright sunlight outside it was pitch black. Ally was afraid. She hated the dark and clutched hold of Signet's cloak more tightly with both hands as she followed him down the tunnel. She remembered back to their last adventure, when Grim and Grisly were chasing them and Vastator was lurking around every corner. She shivered at the memories, glad that she was in the middle. Archie was behind, holding on to her T-shirt, or she might be afraid that something or somebody might creep up and grab her from behind.

"Oh blistering bagwort and squealing snortlefish," Signet cursed loudly as he stumbled over something in the dark. Ally giggled to herself. She liked it when Signet used funny words. "Aha, I can see some light now."

They came round a corner and the narrow passage was suffused with light. Archie and Ally blinked in the sudden brightness.

"Now then, we just carry on down this passage and down some steps and we'll be there."

"How do the lights work?" Archie questioned.

"Well, in ancient times, when the Oosha was first made, we started off with lighted torches in the sconces in the walls. Then one of the wizards discovered a rock, which we eventually called Lumenite, because of its properties. Now who was it? Ah yes, it

1

was Jera. He picked up a piece of this piece of rock because he thought it was attractive. That night while he was cooking his dinner over a fire, he accidentally dropped it into the flames and to his surprise it started to glow and kept glowing even after it was taken out of the fire. Amazing discovery. So we made some torches and fixed the rock into the end, heated them and we've placed them down all of the passages. Incredibly, the light doesn't run out. Well it hasn't yet."

The children were fascinated and stopped to study the torches.

"The light has a sort of golden glow," Ally remarked.

"It gives a different light to electric light bulbs. It's very bright but it seems softer because, as Ally says, it's a golden colour," Archie added.

Signet looked at the two children and smiled. "Come on you two. There's a lot more to see and we've only got a few hours."

Archie looked at Signet inquisitively and asked, "I've never heard of Lumenite. Why don't we use it? It seems better than electricity, and it's natural too, so it wouldn't cause any ecological damage."

Signet looked back at him long and hard. "Hmm, wizards can travel to all sorts of different places that humans haven't discovered yet. Come along now. We're nearly there."

Archie's curiosity was aroused but realising that he was not going to get any further with Signet, he carried on along the passage that sloped downwards and grew wider. Soon they were able to walk three abreast. Ally hadn't seemed to notice Signet's reluctance to talk about Lumenite, so asked, "Can I have a piece of Lumenite for my rock collection?" She carried on, "My friend Zonah has a big collection of different rocks and crystals. I've started my own collection and keep them in a shoebox. It would be good to find a new rock. If you can give me two bits then I can give one to her."

Archie surreptitiously watched Signet's reaction.

"Well, we'll see what we can do," he said, brushing aside Ally's request.

Archie knew that when adults said, "We'll see," in that tone of voice, what they really meant was, "No, but I don't want to explain why and I hope you'll forget about it so I don't have to explain." Archie was even more curious but he said nothing.

Ally took no notice and chattered on. "I like the way it's got a lovely curved ceiling." She was happy now that the tunnel was brightly lit.

The incline of the passage gradually became so shallow they had to take two steps and a hop. Then the steps grew steeper and all held on to the rail in the wall. The stairs opened out into an entrance hall. Archie and Ally saw two enormous wooden doors, with the biggest keyhole that they had ever seen. Their eyes were growing wider by the minute. Signet took a bunch of keys from a clip in his belt and picked out the largest key. He threw open the doors and made an elaborate gesture with his arm as if he were introducing a person.

The children moved into the doorway and gasped in surprise. There was complete silence as they were unable to make another sound. Archie gulped and looked at his sister and noticed that her eyes were like saucers. They kept on staring as if mesmerised. The sanctuary was breathtakingly beautiful.

Signet stood aside and motioned for the children to go in. He said nothing. He was used to this reaction when anyone saw the Oosha for the first time. Archie and Ally walked a little farther inside. It was very large; larger than they both imagined. It had a very tall ceiling. There were pillars on both sides with arches between them. The light and shimmering colours had stunned the children into silence. The whole place glowed.

Archie was the first to recover. "Where does the light come from?"

"Ah, well. We discovered that if we ground the Lumenite up and mixed it with paint then the paint gave off light. We heated up the rock to higher temperatures to make it crumble and we found that according to the temperature used, the rock gave out a different coloured light."

3

"It's so pretty! Look there's red, and yellow and gold, and green. Oh, purple too. It's got all the colours of the rainbow," Ally exclaimed in surprise. She thought for a minute of the rhyme that she had learnt to remember the colours in the rainbow. "What was is it? Oh yes I remember now, Richard of York gave battle in vain. Red, Orange, Yellow, Green, Blue, Indigo and Violet. Look, look, Archie, in between the pillars there is an alcove and each is a different colour." Ally stuttered as she grew more excited. "E—e—each side is the same, and the colours all seem to blend into each other. L—l—look between the orange and yellow. It's kind of gold and between the green and blue its sort of turquoise."

"Oh yes, I see what you mean, Ally, and there's a round table at the top and the colours are all blue, purple and deep pink."

"Magenta," Signet commented. "The colour is called Magenta."

Ally looked around in awe. "It's beautiful. Look at the high-backed chairs around the table. What are they made of Signet? Look at the way they are carved. And ooh, look at the top! There's a larger chair that has more carvings. That must be for a very important person. Who sits on that chair, Signet? Do you sit on it?"

"Wow, look at the floor, Ally! It seems to be made of marble slabs. Oh the ones round the outside must be made of Lumenite because they kind of glow. Look there's a pattern on the floor too. You'd never know that it was underground, it seems so light in here and the air feels fresh as well."

"Aah, you noticed the atmosphere. There is a series of air ducts into the temple and passages."

"It's so calm and peaceful," Ally said dreamily.

The children stayed in the temple happy to just explore and to soak up the ambience.

"Aaahh!" Archie's shout echoed noisily round the chamber.

"Aaaaah!" Ally was jolted her out of her pleasant daydream echoing her brother's yell. "Ooh, Archie, you gave me such a fright I nearly jumped out of my skin."

"Sorry, Ally, but I was excited by this. It looks like a radio transmitter and I've always wanted to have a go on a radio. Breaker, breaker, this is Alpha, Romeo, Charlie, Hotel, Come in. Can I try it, Signet? Is it a radio transmitter? What do you use it for?"

Signet gave him one of his inscrutable looks. "Mmm, that's the Transastromitter, and yes you're quite right it is a kind of radio transmitter. We call it a TAM for short. But come on now, we must go. We'll use the connecting passage, which sweeps down the London Road and ends up under the Old Steine. Remember, I told you that it used to come out at the beach but since the sewage system was installed the end of the passage, it was destroyed. We have a secret door now which links into the sewage system. We'll go that way and then we can go out through the manhole in Steine Gardens."

"Cool," Archie said, "I'd like that."

"It sounds exciting, but I hope the sewage doesn't pong though," Ally said wrinkling her nose.

"No, you'll be alright. The sewage is all chemically treated so there is no smell." Signet reassured her.

They followed Signet out of another door at the other end of the cathedral and gradually began to climb downwards. The passage was wide and well lit with the luminescent lamps, and so they all walked along together, chatting as they walked.

"So what do you use the TAM for then?" Archie asked Signet.

"All in good time, my boy. I'll tell you when it's the right time."

Archie was very, very curious now. First there was the rock Lumenite that seemed to come from a place inaccessible to humans, and now there was this TAM thing. What on Earth was it used for?

Chapter Two

The Tannery

In another galaxy, millions of miles away on the planet Altair, Thorin, the Elf, was happy. He was the owner of the one of the biggest tanneries on Altair and he hummed a tune as he bounded up the stairs to his office and sat back in his chair behind his desk. The reason for his good mood was that it was his son Zegar's birthday and his wife was at home organising a birthday party. Thorin was going to leave work early at three of the morning moon to be at the party to help out.

His secretary, Saskaret popped her head round the door and said questioningly."Celix?"

Thorin smiled at her. "Wonderful, yes a cup of Celix is just what I need."

Saskaret came back minutes later with a steaming cup and Thorin sat back and thought about his current problem in the tannery.

"How's that nephew of yours? How does he like Terra?"

Thorin smiled again at her seemingly innocent remark. He knew that she had a crush on Julektar. Well, if he liked her too, they would make a good match. Come to think about it when Julektar had come home for his mid-Serai break, he had spent a lot of time at the tannery. Thorin had been pleased as he thought he was interested in the business, which was a good thing since Thorin was planning to offer him a position. Thorin remembered

Julektar had turned up at the Tannery with a basket clutched in his arms. Thorin had thought this was a little strange but mentally shrugged his shoulders. Perhaps there was a romance already. He smiled at Saskaret. "You can ask him yourself. He's coming home soon and he's going to be working for me at the tannery."

Saskaret blushed and left the office.

Thorin went back to the problem. The Grilks. The pesky little gnawing animals had somehow got into store rooms next to the tanning yard. This was where they stored the bark of the Tarran tree that they used to make the liquid that rid the hides of fat and hair during the tanning process. The Grilk population had exploded recently and had invaded the tannery. They mostly ate smaller animals but also liked to gnaw at the tarran bark and were becoming a greater nuisance every day. Thorin finished his Celix and went downstairs into the tanning yard to look for Hott, his foreman, to see if the poison had worked. "How are things? Have we got rid of the Grilks?"

"Well, it's very strange. I didn't use the poison because I haven't seen hide nor hair of them. The funny thing is some of the men say they've seen some very large black animals. I've just seen a tail whisk round that corner so we seem to have swapped one pest for another. I've never seen anything like it in my life."

"Perhaps they did us a favour and killed all the Grilks for us. Are these things eating the tarran bark?"

"Well I don't think they like that, but they do seem to be causing some problems. We found a canvas sheet that they had started to gnaw and it looks like they've been having a go at some ropes too."

"We can't have that. You'd better go ahead and put the poison down tonight. Everything else is okay?"

"I was going to come up and see you; a couple of the men went sick yesterday and Quesir is complaining about a sore throat and says he feels feverish."

"Okay, it's probably just the ague. It's that time of year. Keep me informed. It's my son's birthday today so I shall be leaving about three."

"Say Happy Birthday to him from me. How old is he now?"

"He's eleven."

"Goodness, it seems like only yesterday that we were all toasting you on the day he was born. Doesn't time fly? Tch, tch." Thorin started to walk away. "Well you know what they say: as you get older, time seems to pass much quicker."

Chapter Three

A Surprising Appearance

Archie and Ally followed Signet as he squeezed through the small opening. They were smaller and so it was no trouble. They found themselves in a narrow, low-ceilinged passage. Signet had to bend slightly but the two children found that they could walk along quite easily.

"It'll be okay in a minute, the passage widens out and I'll able to walk without bending," Signet said ruefully rubbing his head where he had just bumped it. "This used to be the old sewage system and in Victorian times they enlarged it and so it was blocked off."

They came to what seemed like a dead end with a bricked up entrance. Signet pressed a brick on the wall. An entrance in the brickwork swung open and Signet ushered them through into an enormous chamber. "We had to make a secret entrance," Signet said as he turned and pressed a brick on the wall and the entrance closed up.

"Cool," Archie said.

"Can you open the entrance from this side?" Ally asked.

"Yes, if you count five bricks across from the left and the ten bricks up and press that brick it will open. Watch." Signet counted across and up and pressed the brick and the doorway appeared.

"Wow," Ally gasped in fascination as Signet closed the entrance again. They could hear the sound of rushing water and

Archie and Ally walked round a corner and saw two streams of water merging into one big river.

"It's enormous," Archie said as he let out a whistle.

Ally turned to Signet. "Is that sewage?"

"Yes, they pump it out to Telscombe Cliffs where it is chemically treated before it is flushed out into the sea"

"Ooh, yuck! You mean that's all the poos and wees from everyone in Brighton?"

"Well, it's watered down by all the water from washing machines, dishwashers and bathwater. But yes, all the flushings from toilets are in there too."

"Yuck, I'm never going near it then." Ally shuddered.

"No-one is asking you to, you goose," Archie remarked.

Signet strode ahead leading the way. "Come on now, we just need to go round this corner, up a passageway, and then we'll come to the stairs that lead up to the manhole."

"Oh yes, that's going to be cool coming out in the middle of the Old Steine. I bet everyone will stare and wonder where we've come from," Archie said.

"Yeah, they'll probably think you're an alien!" .

"Oh very funny, Allie, but they'll think you're the alien, not me."

"Shush, you two, I thought I heard some sounds. Quiet for a moment." Signet stopped and held up his hand for the children to stop talking. There was a low murmuring sound as if two people were talking and moving away and then there was silence. Signet cautiously moved towards the corner and peered around it.

"There's no-one there, I expect the sound carries down here. Oh well, come on then."

The children followed Signet around the next turning and bumped into him as he stopped suddenly and said, "Oh spells preserve us, Aloric; you gave me such a fright. What are you doing here?"

Archie and Ally peered around Signet and both gave a sharp

intake of breath. The sound of their gasps echoed eerily around the sewer. Ally opened her mouth to say something but found that no words would come out and she could only stand and stare in open-mouthed amazement. Archie was so stunned at the sight that he didn't even try to speak. The children were speechless for the second time that day.

Chapter Four

Aloric

rchie and Ally blinked in amazement. They could hardly believe their eyes as they saw that a Unicorn stood before them. It was a magnificent animal. It was pure white in colour with a silver horn on its forehead and matching silver hooves. The beautiful creature spoke in a deep melodious voice.

"Greetings, Signet Eolzig, Thank goodness I found you. My mother Asphodel sent me. You must come with me now. We need your help in Altair. There is something very wrong. There is a dreadful plague and many of the Altairians are dying. Asphodel said you must come quickly. The Council have summoned the Seraim tutors from the four planets. They think the disease must have been brought in somehow from one of the planets that we visit."

The children were so amazed at seeing a Unicorn that his words went over their heads. Archie frowned in puzzlement and whispered to Ally, "I thought Unicorns were bigger than that. This one is a bit small. It's only the size of a small pony."

Ally whispered back, "I think he's only young. He said his mother Asphodel sent him."

Signet recovered from his surprise and took charge and in a matter of fact voice introduced the Unicorn to the children. "This is Archie and his sister Ally; they are friends of mine, Aloric.

12

Archie and Ally this is Aloric, the son of Asphodel who is the president of Altair."

"I'm very pleased to meet you," Aloric said, "And yes, Ally, you are right, I am only young, I'm just a two-yearling, which I suppose in your human terms means that I am about twelve or thirteen years. I'm a teenager like you!"

Ally gasped out, "It's lovely to meet you, Aloric. I love Unicorns. I've got loads of books about them at home, but I never thought I would meet a real one."

Archie blushed as he said, "I'm very pleased to meet you too, Aloric. He hadn't meant for Aloric to hear him and he hoped that he wasn't offended.

"No I'm not offended at all. No harm done. You haven't met a Unicorn before so you wouldn't know what size we are." Aloric gave a great laugh.

Archie wondered how he seemed to know what he was thinking. Signet started to pace up and down and mumble to himself. Archie and Ally managed to stop staring at Aloric and looked to Signet.

"Hmm, I was going to get round to telling you about Altair sometime, but it looks like it'll have to be now. Altair is another world in a different galaxy. The magical creatures that you know from your Earth myths and fables live there, like the flower fairies, gnomes, dwarfs, unicorns, ooh too many to mention now. Altair is far more advanced that Earth and the Altairians have the power to space travel. They do not see themselves as unusual; they are just different tribes living in one world. They visit this world from time to time and then go back to Altair, but at times they have been seen on Earth and that has inspired the fairy tales with magical and mythical creatures. I can visit Altair myself using their method of space travel but we made the TAM, as it's easier. You can set it to a different radio frequency and cross to Altair that way."

Archie nodded to himself in satisfaction. He had just known there was some secret about the radio transmitter in the Oosha.

"Now, you two, I am going with Aloric so if you go up that

iron ladder there it will take you out through a manhole into the Old Steine gardens and you can catch a bus home."

"Can't we come too; we might be able to help?

"No, not this time." Signet said, "It could be dangerous. Sometime in the future when this problem is sorted out, then perhaps you can go, but I can't take you this time."

"But what if something happens to you, how will we know?"

"Nothing is going to happen to me. I'm a wizard, don't forget, and I can look after myself."

Ally was reassured, but Archie didn't like to give up that easily. "But what if something happens to us? What if we need you?"

Signet gave a laugh at Archie's persistence. "Troublesome boy, nothing is going to happen to you. Just go straight home and no harm can come to you." Signet looked at Archie for what seemed to be a long while. "Mmm, you still can't come with me. But on second thought, just in case you need some help before I come back, if you think it is urgent, go to the five forked tree in Hollingdean woods. You'll find Rufus there every day at 12 Noon. He'll help you." He pointed his ring at Ally and at Archie in turn and it started to glow. "I endow you with the gift; I place a great deal of trust in you. Use it well."

"What's the gift?" Archie asked.

"It's something you might need," Signet replied. And with that both he and the Unicorn vanished.

Chapter Five

The Epidemic

As soon as Signet and Aloric reached Altair, Aloric took him to the hospital. Doctor Beshley was in charge of the epidemic and when they arrived at her office, the door was open and she was on the communicator.

She motioned for them to come in and they heard her say, "Thorin, I'm sorry to have to tell you that one of your men has just died in the hospital. We couldn't save him. We now have over thirty Elves here complaining of the same symptoms. I'm glad you called as I was going to send someone to order you to close the tannery. We've decided that all the men and women who worked at the tannery and their families will have to go into quarantine, and that includes you and your family, Thorin, with immediate effect. It's the only way to stop this disease. It's spreading like wildfire and at the moment our Doctors and medical staff are baffled by the disease. We have set up a special diagnostics team, to try to come up with some answers." Dr Beshley nodded to Signet acknowledging his presence and switched the communicator to Loudspeaker so that he could hear Thorin's reply.

"Right, I'll send a message out to all my staff and mark it urgent. That way their communicators will keep buzzing until they pick up the message. Now where shall I tell them to go?

"We've evacuated a whole wing of the hospital and when you

report there you will be shown where to go. I'll call in to see you. We have staff there at this moment interviewing everyone who is connected to the tannery to collect as much information as possible. Only then can we sort out some kind of solution."

Doctor Beshley broke the connection and turned to Signet. "Welcome Signet, I'm really glad to see you. This illness is a killer, and we've never seen anything like it before on Altair. It seems to have come from nowhere. We think it may have started in the tannery. I was speaking to Thorin, the owner, and I've just ordered him to close the place down and come to the hospital."

Thorin stared into space as the connection with Doctor Beshley on his communicator ended. He thought glumly that his son Zegar would be disappointed that the planned picnic excursion was cancelled. His musings were interrupted as Hott burst into his office.

"We've got a problem, boss. I've just had a phone call from Melina, the wife of one of the two men who are sick. She said that both of the men have been admitted to hospital. The Doctors don't seem to know what is wrong with them. They're both on life support machines and it looks pretty serious. Melina's daughter is ill as well, and they are all at the hospital."

"Yes, I've just had a call from Doctor Beshley, the head of Epidemics and Communicable Diseases, ordering me to close the tannery. She's told us that everyone who works here and their families will have to report to the hospital and go into quarantine. It makes sense if we have any hope of containing the disease and stopping it from spreading. I'll get Saskaret to make a notice and we'll put it on the gates. Do you feel okay?" Thorin looked at his foreman anxiously.

"Yes, don't worry about me I've got the constitution of a Wokbatt."

Thorin smiled at him to hide the sinking feeling he had in the pit of his stomach. He didn't want to worry Hott with his thoughts. He did not think that this disease was just a new form of ague. He had a horrible suspicion that it was more deadly. The ague he knew, but this seemed somehow different. "All right then, you had just better lock everything up and get yourself and your family to the hospital."

Thorin called Saskaret and told her about the problem. She disappeared into the office workroom where they had all the equipment she needed to produce the large laminated notice to be put on the gate. Thorin sighed as Saskaret came in to his office proudly holding the sign she had made.

"Shall I fix it to the gate as I leave?"

Thorin thanked her and with a heavy heart broke the news to her about the quarantine. He told her that he would take care of the sign.

Saskaret was young and she could not hide her feelings. She looked scared and her face was white with shock. She rushed to retrieve her cloak from its usual peg on the clothes stand in the main office and poked her head round the door. "Bye, Thorin, I'll see you at the hospital then." And she was gone.

Thorin picked up his communicator for the second time. He typed out a message to be sent urgently to his staff to give them the bad news. He put 'All' in the 'To' box and pressed the send command. He then pressed the button connecting him to his home and this time he pressed the picture key. His son's Elven face appeared on the screen. He beamed at him when he recognised his father's face on their home communicator.

"Dad, when are you coming home?"

"Soon, but can you get Mum for me, it's very important."

Zelana's face came into focus on the screen. Some people showed their emotions clearly. Zelana his wife was one of these and he watched her face fall apart as he told her about the disease and the quarantine.

"I'll be home in a short time. Pack a few things to take with us and maybe take some of the food for the picnic we were planning and we can have it at the hospital. I'm sure some of your home cooking will cheer everyone up."

He noticed that his wife had pulled herself together and, always the sensible one, she said, "Okay, Darling. Everything's already packed in the picnic hamper. It might be fun. I shall feel like Lady Bountiful going around and giving out food. Don't worry. I'll organise everything. Don't be long. We'll be ready and waiting for you."

When Thorin and his family arrived at the hospital they were shown to the quarantine wing. It was organised chaos and there seemed to be people rushing here and there. They were shown to a large waiting room. There was a buzz in the air of people talking, sighing, crying and shouting angrily. Thorin looked at his son Zegar proudly; he was a good kid and hadn't made a fuss. In fact, he seemed to be enjoying all the excitement. He didn't seem worried at all. Thorin relaxed and thought, *of course it would all seem like an adventure to him.*

"Shall we get the picnic out?" Zegar asked his Mum.

Thorin and his wife smiled at each other over their son's head, his enthusiasm making them forget about the awful implications of the quarantine for awhile.

"Why not," Zelana replied and the two of them were soon busy laying out all the food on a table. Zelana had thought of everything and had even brought paper plates and soon Zegar was scurrying about distributing the plates and inviting people to come and join the picnic.

Thorin was glad they were occupied as it gave him the opportunity to talk to Doctor Beshley. He had noticed her at once. She was tall and distinguished looking and seemed to be giving out all the orders. Thorin approached her and tapped her on his shoulder

"Doctor Beshley, I'm the owner of the tannery, Thorin. We spoke earlier by communicator.

"Ah yes, come with me," she said and ushered him into a side room.

She asked Thorin a few questions about the tannery and what they used to treat the hides. She seemed interested when Thorin told him that they used vegetable tanning processes and asked him to explain further. Thorin obliged but he did not think it was important to mention the Grilks. His main concern was to ask his own questions about the outbreak and its effects.

Doctor Beshley answered him, "Yes, yes of course you want to know about it. I'll tell you everything that we know. It seems to start with a fever and chills, sore throat, shortness of breath and nausea."

"That doesn't sound too serious. How did poor Shokar die?"

"Well, the unfortunate chap died of pneumonia, the disease seemed to settle on his chest and there was nothing we could do. But that's not all . . . some people are experiencing abdominal pain and gastrointestinal complaints. Now, one of our patients has developed a swollen lymph gland that is quite painful. Another has developed a stiff neck, rather like the start of meningitis. The Doctors here cannot identify the organism that is causing the disease. "

"I see."

"This is why we're asking for any information that you think will help."

"Yes, well, if I think of anything I'll let you know." Thorin was too distracted and worried about his family to consider mentioning the strange long-tailed animals that some of his men had seen in the tannery.

Chapter Six

Eavesdropping

"What's the gift do you think?" Ally asked her brother. Archie pointed his finger at a pebble on the ground. "Change into a Mars bar." Nothing happened and they both started to giggle. Archie shrugged his shoulders. "Well, it's not a spell that will change stones into something edible. But wasn't it awesome, the way they just seemed to disappear into thin air? Anyway, while we're here on our own, we might as well do a bit of exploring before we go out of the manhole. Come on let's just look up this passage."

Ally skipped along behind Archie. "Okay, it's great down here, and I'm not scared 'cos the passageways have all got electric lights. What do you think is down there?"

"Don't know. Let's have a look."

The children had only gone a little way when they became aware of voices. At first it seemed like a distant murmuring which became louder and louder.

"Shh, a minute," Archie whispered to Ally. "There are some men up there. Let's creep up and listen to what they are talking about. It'll be fun."

They crept up closer to the men and stopped just round a corner from them. Archie peeped round at them. He whispered back to Ally, "There are two men in suits holding a map or a plan. I think they must be architects."

"Right, so you've marked the wall with a yellow cross to show you the exact spot. I know that you've already dug a tunnel from there to the bank vault. At 7:30 a.m. you enter the sewers through the manhole. This will give you plenty of time to get to your tunnel and place the explosives that will blast a hole into the bank vault. You set the explosive device to go off at 12:30. You must be in the vault by 12:40 which will give you exactly fifteen minutes to open safety deposit box number 199. You must be out of the vault by 12:55 p.m. as the security guards check the TV screens every half an hour, on the hour and half an hour. The TV cameras scan the boxes but they cannot see the wall, so when you have opened box 199, you must close it. As long as you do this you will be quite safe. Don't even think about opening any of the other boxes. You won't have time. You must be back in the sewer and out of sight by 1:00 p.m."

Archie and Ally looked at each other in amazement. Archie put his finger up to his lips and peeped round the corner at the men. He observed that the one who was doing all the talking was very sun-tanned and somehow looked affluent. He was wearing an expensive looking suit and had short cropped hair. He looked neat and tidy. Archie thought from his tone of his voice and the way he spoke in curt clipped words that he was some sort of military man. He reminded him of Jazz's friend, the Colonel, whom he and Ally had met one day when they visited Jazz.

"I'll tell you now how the handover of the goods will take place. There will be no further contact with Mr. M or myself. You will enter and exit the sewer through the manhole in Steine gardens and we will make sure it is unlocked. We've arranged to put a builder's tent around it so that people won't see you coming and going. You will carry out this operation the day after tomorrow on Saturday when the Brighton Festival and Parade is taking place. All the crowds and the police will be at the other end of Brighton. Security box number 199 will contain a couple of Faberge eggs which are priceless. It will be in the security box for one day only as they are on the way to an exhibition in London.

21

Mr. M has a buyer who has put in an order for these works of art. Mr. M will pay you £100,000 in sterling. You will park your car in Safeway's car park. There's a pay meter for parking and I want you to buy something, so that you have the supermarket's own carrier bag, which we shall need."

The other man spoke for the first time. "Yeah, how do I hand over the goods and get my money?"

Archie peered around the corner and looked at the other man. He couldn't see him as well as he was behind the other man. He noticed that he was a little taller and as he moved into view Archie noticed that he was not so well dressed. He spoke with an American accent. He was older than the other man and Archie noticed that he had white hair and thought he looked a bit of a rough diamond.

The military man carried on in his clipped voice. "You will reach Safeway by 1:15 and you have fifteen minutes to buy something at Safeway, which will allow you to exit the car park. You will exit Safeway at 1:30 and you have thirty minutes to drive to the Marina and park. We will make the exchange at the UCA cinema at the Marina at 2:15. Place the boxes containing the goods in the Safeway's carrier bag and put it down by the side of the drinks machine near the sweet counter." He handed a large envelope to the other man. "Mr. M has given you £50,000 in advance and when I have the eggs I will arrange for the transfer of the balance of your money to your bank account. I have details of the sort code and account number, which you have already given me. Mr. M has a yacht at the Marina and we sail at high tide that same evening. So as long as everything goes to schedule, the eggs will be out of the country and delivered to the buyer before the robbery has even been discovered. Now, I think that covers everything. You can take this map of the sewage system and I have marked the spot where you must drill into the bank vaults. Have you got any further questions? Is everything quite clear?"

Archie tiptoed backward away from the men and gestured to Ally to do the same. When they had gone back a few feet they turned and ran on tiptoe. When they were out of the men's earshot, Ally whispered to her brother, "It's just like last time, why do we always seem to overhear plots?"

Archie whispered back, "No, it's worse. These men are extremely dangerous, compared to them, Grim and Grisly were amateurs. We'd better get out of here quickly, before they discover us. Come on, Ally, the ladder to the manhole is just round this corner."

As the two children reached the corner they jumped in fright as they saw a dark shape bending over a grille.

"Come on, my little darlings, back you go."

Archie and Ally stood mesmerised by the sight before them. It was Vastator and he was taking rats from a cage on the floor, holding each one by its tail as he dropped them back into the sewer. As they turned back, Ally noticed that the cage still had a few writhing black rats.

Ally vaguely heard shrill voices shouting, *"Let me out too, I'm not your little darling. I don't want to be in this cage,"* but she was too busy running after Archie to pay any attention. They reached the large chamber where the two streams ran into one large river of sewage.

"What are we going to do now, Archie?"

"There's another way out that leads to under the pier. Come on, we need to go up this spiral staircase."

Just at that moment the children heard the voices of the men coming down the corridor and they could hear Vastator's steps coming down the other passage. Ally was terrified,

"Oh no Archie, what can we do? We haven't got time to get up the staircase. They'll see us. We're trapped."

Archie looked around. "Come on quick, Ally. We'll just have to hide in the sewer. If we go up that ladder up the concrete bank and down the other side into the water, we can hang on to the ladder and we won't be seen. You can't see over the concrete bank unless you stand on the special ledge. Come on quick."

Ally was horrified. "I can't go into the sewer. There are lumps of poo floating about and rats swimming around. I j—j—j—just can't."

"Come on, Ally, you'll have to. There's nowhere else to hide. Just close your eyes."

Ally looked towards Vastator's voice. Then she turned her head towards the echoes of the voices of the men getting louder as they walked along the other passage. She hesitated for a second, held her nose and then followed Archie up the ladder and down the other side.

Chapter Seven

Sewer rats

"Wow, we're lucky. Look, Ally, there's a kind of ledge here that's hidden from the outside."

As Ally came over the iron stairs she could see Archie scrambling on to the ledge. She breathed a sigh of relief, but still held her nose as she stepped across onto the narrow shelf and crouched out of sight under the overhang. She peered down into the murky water of the sewer flowing past under the ledge and gave a shudder. She was sure she could see all sorts of dark shapes floating in the water. Were they lumps of something revolting, or even worse, were they rats swimming past? She turned to Archie and put her hand on her heart and said, "Whew."

Archie held his finger up to his lips. He could feel his heart pounding even though he knew that they were safely out of sight. They could hear the men talking as they walked towards them from one passage and Vastator's footsteps echoed eerily as he approached from the other direction. Archie mouthed to Ally, "Keep very still." He was worried. Vastator might be able to detect them with his extra sensory powers. He was a loose cannon. You never knew what he might do. Ally squeezed her eyes tightly shut and drew her knees up to her chest. She let go of her nose and put her arms around her knees. She tried to make herself as small as possible.

They heard Vastator stop and then there was silence as if he too were listening to the two men. Archie held his breath and both he and Ally kept as still as statues. The two men were completely unaware that there was anyone else in the sewers and were talking and laughing as they made their way up the passage and up the iron staircase that led to the manhole exit. There was complete silence.

Ally opened her eyes. She looked at Archie and opened her mouth to speak. Archie clamped his hand over her mouth quickly and shook his head. He pointed in Vastator's direction and then put his fingers to his lips, Ally nodded and he took his hand away. They both crouched there on the ledge hardly daring to breathe. Then they heard Vastator moving towards them. Archie could see Ally's eyes growing rounder and bigger in fear and he put his arm around her. He bit his lip when to his horror he heard Vastator climbing up on a ledge and leaning over the sewer wall. Archie and Ally thought he had discovered their hiding place and they kept as still as possible. Then Vastator began to talk and they realised that he was oblivious to their presence and absorbed in his own business.

"There you are my little beauties. Your brothers and sisters have done the work so I don't need you. You are free."

There was a scraping noise as he tipped the cage over the ledge and a splash and lots of squeaking as the rats hit the water.

"Thanks to you, my little angels of death, my plan is working."

"What's he doing?" Ally mouthed silently to Archie.

Archie shrugged exaggeratedly and they both listened. "Rats." Archie mouthed in reply to Ally. Ally shuddered.

Then to their relief they heard Vastator's steps walking away down the passage, talking to himself as he marched along. The children heard him say, "I'll soon be off to Altair, to be given a hero's welcome. The Philosopher's Stone will be mine and I will be the most powerful being on Earth." Vastator gave an evil laugh, which seemed to echo round the chamber long after he had left. Then there was silence again.

After a minute, Archie leaned across to the iron ladder and

cautiously climbed. He peeked over the sewer wall and then motioned to Ally to follow him. "I think everyone's gone," he whispered. "Come on, let's go."

The pair ran on tiptoe down the passage, which led to the manhole exit. They climbed the long iron ladder as fast as their legs would carry them. They pushed up the manhole cover and came out into the bright sunlight of Steine gardens; they closed the cover behind them and paused to catch their breath. They were both panting with the effort and their hearts were racing as they thought of their narrow escape. A street busker passed them and eyed them up and down with surprise,

"Man, where did you two spring up from? You weren't here a minute ago. Man, you appeared like magic."

Archie and Ally just grinned at the man and started to walk across the gardens into the bus stop. The busker watched them go with a look of amazement. They looked back at him and laughed conspiratorially as they saw him shake his head.

When they arrived home Archie went straight upstairs to his bedroom. Ally made for the kitchen shouting up to him as she went, "I'll get us both a drink, I'm dying of thirst."

Charlie, the cat wrapped himself around her legs. She heard a voice in her head,

"*I'm hungry.*" She looked at Charlie in astonishment and picked him up

"*Mmm, warm*"

"Are you talking to me?"

"*Of course I am.*"

"B—b—b but you've never done this before."

"*I have, but you just didn't hear me.*"

Ally put Charlie down on the kitchen worktop. She opened the cupboard took out a tin of cat food. She picked up Charlie's bowl from the floor, opened the tin and put half of it into the bowl. She replaced the bowl on the floor and Charlie leapt gracefully from the worktop to the floor.

"*Mmmm, my favourite, tuna fish. Thank you, Ally.*"

Ally replied almost in a trance, "You're welcome." She took the two cans of Coke out of the fridge and ran up the stairs to Archie's room. "Archie, Archie, I think Charlie has just spoken to me."

Archie replied dismissively, "You must have imagined it. Come on we need to talk about everything that has happened and to decide on a plan."

Ally swallowed hard. She knew she wasn't imagining anything, but she agreed with Archie that they needed to work out what was going on.

"Vastator seems to have collected and used rats from the sewer for some purpose. I think we need to let Signet know, as I'm sure it has something to do with the trouble in Altair. Maybe I could use the TAM and go to Altair to warn Signet," Archie said.

Ally nodded in agreement. "But you don't know how to use it," she mused. "We'll just have to go to Hollingdean woods and ask Rufus for help. Signet told us he would help us and he surely knows how to use the TAM. Wait, I've got a brilliant idea, my friend Zonah lives right by Hollingdean woods. I'll ask Mum if we can go to her house tomorrow. Then I'll ring Zonah and ask if it will be okay if we both come over for the day. I wonder who Rufus is and what he looks like," Ally continued, "and what shall we do about the men who are going to rob the bank?"

Archie pondered, "Well we can't very well go to the police as they will want to know where we overheard them and it'll be difficult to explain how we got into the sewers."

"We could make an anonymous call,"

Archie thought for a minute. "Yes, but would the police believe it? You heard what the men were saying about the alarm going off and the police being called and thinking it was a false alarm. They might just think it was a hoax call and do nothing. Anyway we don't want the Police running around the sewers and investigating tunnels. They might find the secret tunnel to the Oosha."

"Yes I suppose you are right. But we have to do something."

Archie thought for a moment and said, "Well, we know where they are handing over the loot at the Marina cinema at 2.15. They don't know us and we could just pick up the bag and hand it in to the Security men at the cinema and tell them to contact the Police because it contains a valuable item."

Ally brightened. "Yes, that's a good idea. It's the Brighton Festival Parade and we were going to the park anyway so I suppose we can slip away for an hour without too much trouble. I'll go and find Mum and then I'll ring Zonah."

Archie brightened up too. Zonah was very pretty with her long chestnut curls and she was interesting and fun. He liked Zonah and was looking forward to seeing her again.

Chapter Eight

Vastator's plan

Vastator had been so absorbed in his task that he was not aware of the children's presence. They did not know how lucky they had been. His extra sensory powers had picked up human vibrations but he attributed this feeling to the two men who had come down the passage.

He walked back along the passage and teleported out of the sewer to a coffee bar in the Lanes. He bought a coffee and sat outside in the summer sunshine. It was pleasant sitting in the sun, and he always revelled in the feeling of the sun on his face and arms. It was especially moving for him, contrasting vividly with his dark times when he was drawn back to the black abyss where there was no warmth or daylight. He allowed his thoughts to drift back to that fateful day, some months earlier, in the Library at Sussex University when he first met Julektar, or Julian, as he called himself on Earth.

It was pure chance that had taken him to the Library at that particular time and that particular day. He wanted to find more information on the Philosopher's Stone. Although he had talked in person to many Alchemists, he had the niggling thought that there might be something he had missed that would lead him to this stone. Vastator had been bending down to look at the bottom shelf in the section on mythology.

A young man carrying a pile of books so high that he couldn't see over them had tripped over him. The books had scattered everywhere. The young man had blushed with embarrassment, giving profuse apologies. Vastator had said that it was quite alright and no harm had been done and had bent down to help him pick up the books. As he did so, he had noticed that they were all on the subject of Alchemy in the middle Ages, his special interest.

He had looked at the young student with interest and noticed that he was not picking up human vibrations from this person at all. He certainly was *not* human although he looked just like all the other students. He was wearing a pair of jeans and a T-shirt and a hat pulled down over his ears. Vastator had been intrigued and he remembered how he had held out his hand to introduce himself. "Pleased to meet you, I'm Professor Vee and I see we have an interest in common."

The student had juggled with the books and held out his hand awkwardly. "Pleased to meet you, Sir, I'm Julian."

They had shaken hands and went over to a table where Julian was able to put the books down. Vastator had pulled out two seats and they both sat down. He had begun to talk to him about the various Alchemists he had met.

Julian had been fascinated, and had said something like, "Gosh, you must have read a lot to know all of this. I could use your help with my studies."

Vastator had smiled, and replied, "Oh no, I haven't read much at all, I mean that I spoke to them when they were alive."

Julian's eyes had widened. "How is that? I don't understand."

Just at that moment a Librarian filing books on a shelf, in one of the stacks had peered round the corner angrily at hearing voices. She looked as if she was about to tell them off but when she saw Vastator she had said instead, rather deferentially, "Excuse me, professor, but we usually discourage talking in the Library. Would it be possible to carry on with your conversation outside?"

Vastator had given her his most dazzling smile and apologised.

Her anger had melted away, as he had intended, and she had smiled back at him, and said helpfully, "The student bar is just down the steps and to the right."

Julian had grinned ruefully at Vastator and they had nodded in agreement, stood up, and headed for the exit and the students' bar.

Vastator did not usually encourage friendship. He had learned over the many eons of his existence that it was not worth it. Either the friend died in what seemed to him to be but a moment, or when his bright time ended and when he was summoned back to Earth again by the resonance of evil, he found that his friend was no longer alive. It had left him with a feeling of emptiness on many occasions and he had resolved not to make friends. Vastator was lonely. He regarded human beings as insignificant ants, but if there was one thing he did envy it was their ability to have relationships, and much more importantly their determination in questing for their special particular Grail. That, he admired because he too had his own Grail.

As he had walked across the grass to the student bar, Vastator had been taking advantage of a rare opportunity to enjoy the company of a friend. Not only this, but they had a common interest and in Vastator's Machiavellian mind he had thought Julian might help him in his quest for the Philosopher's Stone. Julian would somehow bring him nearer his own precious Grail.

He remembered asking Julian what he would have to drink, and he had replied, "A pint of beer, please. This research is thirsty work."

Vastator had replied, "Good choice, I'll have the same. Two pints of whatever you have on draught please, barman. Thank you."

They had found a vacant table and sat down. Julian had pulled off his hat and ruffled his hair, but not before Vastator had noticed that he had rather long pointed ears. He had thought to himself that he had been right, this was no human. He was an Elf.

Julian had looked at Vastator quizzically, "What did you mean, when you said you had spoken with the Alchemists?"

Vastator had weighed up the situation. He did not usually reveal his true identity but as his new friend was no more a human than he was, he had looked at him directly and said,

"I'm an immortal and I have lived for many thousands of years. I was most interested in the Philosopher's Stone that the Alchemists were trying to discover, so I used to speak with them whenever I could."

Julian's eyes were wide and he had said excitedly, "Why you must know Signet Eolzig, He's an immortal too! I've met him on my home planet Altair. Do you know him?"

Vastator had been taken by surprise and his eyes had narrowed while he carefully considered his reply. Aware that he risked alienating Julian if he admitted that he was an old adversary, he had replied instead, "Why, yes I know him well. He's an old friend of mine. What is he up to these days?"

"He visits us on Altair from time to time. He supervises all the Seraim, like me, during their stay on Terra and reports and liaises with the Council. He visits us all the time and he replenishes his supply of Theolite."

Vastator was used to keeping cool and calm in many difficult situations, but he had hardly been able to hide his excitement.

"Ah, yes, of course Theolite. Just remind me, it has many different properties, isn't that right?"

"Yes, we use it for space travel. It can scramble subatomic particles, send them across radio waves and reassemble them across vast distances."

Julian's words had hit Vastator like a bolt of lightning. This Theolite must be the very Philosopher's Stone. All these years he had been looking for it on Earth, he had been looking in the wrong place. Vastator had begun to question Julian carefully and arranged to meet him the next day on the pretext of helping him with his studies of medieval times.

He smiled as he remembered the way in which his cool and

logical thought processes had helped him to formulate his plan. He had started by asking himself, *How can I get hold of this Theolite, or Philosopher's Stone? It is readily available on Altair, but how can I get there? I can teleport on Earth, but space travel is beyond my capabilities. I know from my conversation with the Elf that I would not be welcome on his planet. Altairians visit other planets themselves, but they did not encourage visitors to their planet, let alone immigrants. I could try to persuade Julian to take me to his planet. But what then? I could ask the Altairians for some Theolite, but why should they give me some of their precious stone? I could threaten them, but they are such an advanced civilisation that this ploy would probably not work.*

No, if I want to get to Altair and obtain some Theolite, I will have to have a lever, something with which to bargain. If I can terrify them in some way and then save them, the Altairians would be certain to show their gratitude and grant me whatsoever reward I desire. And if I desire anything, I desire some Theolite. Now, how can I frighten them, and how can I gain a hold over Julian?

Vastator had thought more about the problem, *This Altair, is clearly more advanced than Earth, but Earth may hold dangers for Altairians that Earth, with its lesser technology, has already solved, but of which, Altair knows nothing. I think I now know what is to be done. I am, after all, an expert on catastrophes.*

Vastator came out of his reverie of the past, back to the present. He relaxed back in his chair, enjoying the feeling of the sun on his face. He was happy and he smiled to himself. As he sipped his coffee in the warm sun, Vastator daydreamed of how pleasant it would be if he could live on Altair. Maybe the curse of only being able to stay alive when the vibrations of evil were present would not work on Altair. It was just possible that he could stay alive in the warm and the brightness forever. Would he still be immortal, or would he become mortal and die like everyone else? He was not frightened of death. In fact, he thought that it might be quite pleasant to grow old and die. Being immortal was incredibly lonely. If only there was someone he could ask. But no-one would know the answer to these questions. He was alone. There was no-one.

Still, he had thought, *he would not need to live on Altair. If he could get the Altairians to give him some Theolite, he could stay quite happily on Earth.* He was absolutely sure that this Theolite was the Philosopher's Stone that the Alchemists had talked about. Why, with just one piece of Theolite, he would be able to make enough gold to be the richest man on Earth. Not that Vastator particularly cared about being rich. No, it was the power that the money would give him that he wanted. He would be able to fund wars, start famines, support terrorists, any number of activities that would ensure the resonance of evil necessary to keep him alive.

He remembered the time when the idea had come to him and he smiled to himself. The first part of his plan had been easy. It had only meant a brief visit to Kosovo and a visit to the sewers and after a few days he was ready to put the plan into operation. The hard part had been to fool Julian with a plausible story so that he would be willing to help him. Without the Elf's help, the plan would not work, and Vastator knew that Julian would never knowingly take any action that would harm Altair. Vastator did not feel guilty about using his new found friend in this way. He did not care if it caused trouble for Julian. It was not that he was immoral but rather he was *amoral* and he just had no conscience whatsoever.

It had been tricky, but Vastator had succeeded in recruiting the Elf's help. Everything was working the way that Vastator had planned. He sat back in the sun, the smile on his distinguished face making him look handsome. Two young girls walked past and one of them nudged the other, pointing her chin towards him. Vastator was in such a good mood that he winked at the girls and they went on their way glancing back at him every now and then. Vastator positively beamed. He could afford to relax now. He had devised a clever plan and everything had fallen into place. His whole potential future had changed. His dimension, for the first time ever, broke out of the mere boundaries of Earth. His Grail now lay in the galaxies and his future looked bright.

Chapter Nine

Rufus

Zonah called out to her mother from the front door, "Mum, we're just going over to the Hollingdean Swing Park. We won't be long,"

"Okay, but be back for lunch at one," her Mum's disembodied voice called back from the kitchen.

The children ran down the road and crossed into the Park. They went around the swings and slides hemmed in by railings and down a narrow path into the woods.

"Have you seen a tree with five branches?" Archie asked Zonah.

"Oh yes, I think it's down here," Zonah replied over her shoulder as she took a path which bent to the left.

"It was hit by the hurricane in 1987 and it's never grown again. It's like a skeleton. Is that where you've got to meet this person?"

"Rufus. Yes, Signet told us he was always there at midday."

"Strange that someone should always be there at the same time each day," Zonah commented.

"Well perhaps he always takes his dog for a walk at that time," Ally said.

The children came to a small clearing where several paths met and in the middle was a tree with five branches.

"Spooky," Ally said.

Just at that moment she jumped in amazement as she could

see a fox walking down the path towards them. She was so surprised that she addressed the fox,

"Hello, what are you doing here?"

The fox sat down in front of the children and looked at them quizzically. "*I was looking for you,*" he said,

"You can talk!" exclaimed Ally and Archie.

Zonah just stared. Her two friends seemed to be talking to some invisible person. She turned round to look behind her but saw no-one. She was bewildered. Were they talking to the fox? Ally noticed her friend's puzzled expression and put her arm round her shoulders.

"Are you speaking to that fox? I can't hear him replying to you, but you seem to be able to hear him?"

Ally looked at her friend and realised what Signet had meant by the gift. She laughed. "It was Signet; he cast a spell before he left. We didn't know what the spell did, but I think we've just found out."

"*If your friend touches you, she'll be able to hear and talk to me.*"

Zonah nodded her head and grinned delightedly. "I can hear you."

Ally slipped her arm from Zonah's shoulders and held her hand so that contact was not broken. "Are you Rufus?" Ally questioned in a hesitant voice.

"*That's right, and you must be Archie and Ally. Signet sent me a message to look out for you.*"

Archie found his voice and stepped forward. "Pleased to meet you, Rufus. We came to find you. You see, Signet was showing us all the underground passages and suddenly Aloric appeared. He came to tell Signet that there was a terrible disease in Altair that was killing off all the population, so he's gone back to Altair with Aloric to see what he can do. We were supposed to go straight home but we hung around for a while and we saw Vastator. Well, we hid and watched him and we think he has got something to do with the disease that's killing everyone in Altair."

"Yes, I see. Hmmm, He's usually the source of all troubles. What is he up to this time?"

"Well it was a bit garbled, but we heard him talking to himself and saying something about the rats had done their job well, and that he was going to Altair. Oh yes, and he would have the Philosopher's Stone, which would make him really powerful. So you see it's really urgent that I let Signet know. Can you get a message to him?"

"I can do better than that. I know how to use the TAM in the Temple, so I can send you to Altair and you can tell Signet yourself. I don't know what Vastator is up to, but we must try to stop him."

Archie brought his hands up and then rolled them into fists punching the air as if he was fighting an invisible enemy. "Biff, bang, take that you worm. We outwitted Vastator the last time we met him, and we must stop him this time. I hate him. I'd like to beat him to a pulp."

A raucous laugh broke out and the two girls clutched each other in fright. There was a flurry of wings and a white parakeet landed on the lowest branch of the tree.

"Don't you know, you silly boy, that you can't beat Vastator? The Dark Lord always wins. He's indestructible. What are you going to do? You're just a scrap of a boy. he's very powerful and evil. You're no match for him."

Ally gave a sigh of relief, "I thought it was Vastator spying on us. Whew, thank goodness it's just a parrot."

The parakeet ruffled her feathers.

"I'm not an it, thank you very much. And another thing, I'll have you know I'm not a parrot. I'm a parakeet." The parakeet fluffed up her plumage making her appear larger. *"I am Clytemnestra, the leader of the white parakeets that inhabit this wood."*

Ally stepped forward, "Hello, I'm Ally. I'm pleased to meet you, Clytemnestra. I've heard that there was a group of parakeets that lived in Hollingdean woods, but we thought you had all died in the hurricane."

The parakeet seemed mollified by the respect in Ally's voice.

"I am pleased to meet you too, Ally. You can call me Nessie. My owners gave me this rather pretentious name, but I prefer to shorten it."

Ally bombarded Nessie with questions tumbling out of her mouth like a jet of water from a tap. "How did you come to l—l— live in these woods? Don't you find it a bit cold? I mean you're used to a hotter climate. How did you learn to understand English and how can you speak so well?"

Rufus spoke before Nessie could answer, *"Nessie escaped and found her way to these woods back in the 80's. She managed to survive on berries and worms and as she was much bigger than the native birds, they left her alone. But she was a bit lonely and then one day as she was singing, she heard an answering call singing out the same notes. She flew to where the sound was coming from and she saw another parakeet. She was overjoyed and flew to his side. Well that was it, and it was love at first sight. They mated and had a family and the group just grew from there. There are about twenty-five in the flock now, or is it twenty-six, Nessie?"*

"There are twenty-six of us now." Nessie puffed out her feathers proudly and fixed her beady eyes on Archie.

Archie was wondering why everyone was making such a fuss of the parakeet when she had just insulted him. He glared back at her and gave her an exaggerated salute. "Pleased to meet you too, Nessie. Are you always so rude to people?"

"My dear boy I just speak my mind."

Rufus could see that Archie was angry and diplomatically stepped in quickly. *"Now I expect you kids have to be home for lunch, so I'll meet you at two and I'll show you how to use the TAM. Will that be alright?"*

Ally had also noticed Archie's mood and quickly took the lead from Rufus. Taking Archie's arm and pulling him, she said over her shoulder, "Okay. That's fine Rufus. We'll be here. Come on, Zonah, or we'll be late for lunch and your Mum will be cross."

The three children hurried off.

Chapter Ten

The T.A.M

A rchie greeted Rufus as he skidded down the path and hurtled to a standstill. He looked around and felt relieved that the parakeet was nowhere to be seen. He didn't need to be put down by a parrot. Ally and Zonah interrupted his thoughts as they caught up with him at the tree.

"Hi, Rufus."

"Good afternoon to you all. Well now that you are here, we'll go to the temple. I've got a shortcut down to the London Road Tunnel and we'll use that and then we can cut through to the temple itself."

The children followed Rufus to the top of the incline and crawled after him as he disappeared under a large bush. They reached a small clearing which was invisible from the outside.

"Oh, wow! This would make a great camp," Archie said as he looked around.

Rufus pushed on a large rock and it rolled to one side, revealing a large hole in the ground where it had been resting.

"This is one of the air vents which keep the tunnels and temple ventilated. We maintain these vents for Signet. There's a travelator that we use for maintenance. It's quite large as we carry tools in it," Rufus explained as he pulled out a strange looking contraption from the entrance to the tunnel. *"There's plenty of room so we can all fit in."*

The travelator was like a sledge with wheels and high sides. As the children scrambled into it, they felt quite safe. The little raised seats covered with cushions were comfortable and the sides gave them a feeling of security.

When they were all settled, Rufus turned to them and said, *"Keep your heads below the sides and you'll be quite safe. The tunnel is always about a foot higher than the sides. Now we'll start off slowly at first and then the tunnel goes round a corner and dips quite steeply before it levels off. Is everybody Okay? Then off we go."*

Ally who was a little afraid of the dark whispered to Zonah, "It's a bit like the ghost train on the Pier. I feel as if something is lurking in the dark ready to jump out at us."

Zonah chuckled. "Well, my Mum says that they employ someone to stand in the Ghost train 'cos last time I went on it I got tickled by a feather duster and slapped round the face with a wet codfish, least that's what it felt like, but my Mum said it was probably a wet flannel."

Ally giggled and felt reassured and as the little cart picked up speed, she had no more time to be worried. Archie let out a whoop as they went round the bend and started to descend rapidly. Ally quickly recovered from her fears and soon they were all yelling with delight. They sped down the tunnel and as it levelled out, the cart slowed down and shimmied to a stop.

"Wow what a ride," Archie said as he jumped out of the cart. The girls scrambled out after him laughing in agreement.

The tunnel had come to an abrupt end and there was nothing but a stone wall facing them. There was a grille in the earth floor and they all crowded around Rufus as he peered down. The light was very dim, but they could just see another tunnel and they could hear the faint sound of water swishing.

"How do we get down there?" Archie asked.

"Hold on, I've got to check that it's safe first." Rufus put his nose to the grille and sniffed and then he made a great show of twitching his whiskers.

The girls giggled, and as Rufus carried on sniffing and clowning around Archie began to laugh too.

"OK, there's no-one around." Rufus proclaimed

"Not even Vastator?" Allie asked anxiously.

"Especially not Vastator."

"That's good he's . . . well radical," Zonah piped up with a giggle.

The other two joined her in her laughter. Rufus lifted the grille with one paw and used his teeth to grab the rope ladder, which was concealed in a cavity in the stone wall. He used his mouth and teeth and quickly attached the two clip hooks at one end of the ladder to the grille and threw it down into the murky depths of the sewer.

"You three go down the ladder and then I'll pull it up and put it back in its place. I'll follow you down. Shut the grille after me. There are a few ledges and paw holds in the sewer wall so I can scramble down."

In no time they were all safely down on what appeared to be a narrow walkway next to the running water of the sewer. Ally had no time to even think about the sewer water as Rufus led the way at a fast pace. Soon they arrived at a familiar spot that Archie and Ally recognised.

"The entrance to the tunnel that leads up to the Oosha is here, Zonah," Archie explained.

Ally counted the number of bricks along and up and pressed hard. Archie and Ally grinned when they saw Zonah's look of amazement and the secret door opened.

"Wait till you see the Oosha. You really will be amazed then."

Rufus carried on leading the group, and Archie and Ally exchanged conspiratorial glances as they approached the temple.

When they reached the door of the temple, Archie and Ally went through first, stood aside and turned to Zonah and said, "Ta-dah!"

Zonah looked at them both. "What, why are you staring at me?"

"We just want to see the expression on your face," Ally said smiling at her friend.

They were not disappointed as Zonah went through the same look of astonishment that they had both felt when Signet had showed them the magical Oosha. Rufus brushed past them and Archie and Ally followed him. Zonah was still awestruck and Archie, who felt that he was an old hand, turned to her nonchalantly and said, "Come on Zonah, I'll show you around."

When Archie and Ally had shown Zonah all the wonders in the temple and she had exclaimed, "Wow!" for the twentieth time, Rufus cleared his throat. *"Harrumph, I hate to interrupt you, but we have got to attend to a rather pressing matter."*

The children gathered around him as he touched various buttons on the TAM and it sprung into life. During lunch, the children had already devised a plan that Archie should go to Altair to warn Signet about Vastator and the rats. Zonah had asked her Mum and organised a sleep over. This would provide the perfect cover if Archie was delayed. Tomorrow was the day of the Brighton Festival parade, which ended at Preston Park where there were stalls, eating places and a Fairground. The children had asked if they could go to the Festival in the park and both sets of parents had agreed that as the venue was very near to Zonah's, it seemed like a sensible idea that they should sleep over at her house the night before.

"Stand here Archie." Rufus pointed to a circle of light that the TAM was creating on the marble floor.

"Good luck." Ally gave her brother a hug. "I can't wait till you come back and you can tell us what it's like in Altair."

Zonah kissed Archie on the cheek and he blushed. Luckily for him, no-one noticed because at that moment Rufus pressed a button and he disappeared.

Chapter Eleven

Altair

Archie, to cover his red face, opened his mouth to answer Ally, but could not speak as his senses exploded into a kaleidoscope of flashing colours. He blinked to clear his head and when he opened his eyes he was alone. He patted himself down. Reassured that he was in one piece, he felt a rush of exhilaration. He knew he must be in Altair and this was going to be an exciting adventure.

He was standing in a meadow of long grass dotted with a profusion of flowers. Some of these seemed to be fluorescent, shimmering in the sunlight. The air was scented and it reminded Archie of the night scented stocks his father had planted in their garden last year. It felt warm and a slight breeze ruffled Archie hair. He could hear strange sounds of whirring, shrieking, unearthly like nothing he had ever heard before. He squinted up at the sky to see if he could identify the source of these sounds. To his surprise, he could see a moon in the sky at one side of the sun in the vivid blue sky.

Behind him was a vast mountain range which disappeared into clouds. In front of him, fields sloped down to a city nestling in a sandy cove. The sea in the distance was a brilliant turquoise colour and it sparkled in the sunshine. He could see beaches of golden sand and could just make out what looked like Unicorns frolicking and playing on the sand. Some were having races along the water's edge and kicking up spray and some were having mock battles. There seemed to be children playing too and some of them were paddling or swimming in the sea. There was a road running down to the city lined here or there with small cottages and strange looking dwellings.

It looked like planet Earth, but it seemed different somehow. The air was clearer and everything seemed to be much brighter and more alive. Archie just stood there and said, "Wow." He shook his head in amazement and said, "Wow" again. He heard a rustling noise in the grass and some giggling and looked towards the noise. His eyes widened as he saw what appeared to be two small girls dressed as fairies. They were dainty and had a fragile look about them. Their dresses and wings reminded him of his sister's fairy costume, but as he looked closer, he could see that these weren't dressing up clothes. Their wings were real and shimmered with a myriad of colours. They were real Fairies!

"Wow!" he said once again. "You're real live Fairies."

They both giggled again and whispered to each other, Archie couldn't make out what they were saying but he knew it wasn't English. Then one stepped forward and shyly asked, "Are you a human bean?"

"Human being, silly. We learned that in Year One. "

"Yes, I'm human and my name's Archie. Pleased to meet you," he said as he held out his hand. They both stepped forward hesitantly and shook his hand.

"I'm called Melix."

"I'm Xandria." The other one said. "We're not allowed to visit Terra yet as we're too young. We've learnt to speak English, but we still need to learn a lot of stuff yet and we go to school every day. It's so boring." And she gave a yawn.

"I know what you mean." Archie grinned.

They both giggled again.

"Are you a boy Terran or a girl Terran?" Melix asked,

"I'm a boy."

There was a distant clanging of a bell.

"Oops, we'll have to go now. That's the after lunch school bell. We'll have to run or we'll be late." Xandria said starting to run towards a small pavilion in the distance.

Melix called out wistfully over her shoulder, "Will you still be here when we come back from school? We'd like to see you again 'cause we've never met a boy Terran before."

Archie called back, "I don't think I shall still be here, but I hope we can meet again."

Archie's thoughts turned back to the reason he had come to Altair. He knew that Signet was somewhere in that beautiful city shimmering in the distance. He had to find him quickly. He had to tell him about Vastator. He had wasted enough time admiring the scenery and becoming orientated. His heart beat faster when he thought of the urgency of his mission. He set off running towards the road that led to the City. When he reached the road, he was concentrating so hard on climbing down the bank and jumping over the ditch that he very nearly landed on top of a small man.

"Jurgen Sast, Ka te see."

Archie looked bewildered as he hadn't understood a word and said hesitantly, "Hello, do you speak English?"

"Of course Oi do. How silly of me, Oi can see you're a Terran boy. Oi'm forgettin' me manners so Oi am. Me name's Zeedah in Altair, but Oi like me earth name better. So here Oi am now. I'm Fingal the Leprechaun, at your service."

Archie studied the man as he replied. He was dressed all in green from top to toe. He had a green waistcoat over a darker green shirt and breeches that came just below his knees. The rest of his legs were covered with green socks and he was wearing a pair of green shoes with silver buckles. His outfit was completed with a green tricorner hat, which he swept off as he introduced himself.

"I'm pleased to meet you, Fingal. My name's Archie and I'm on my way to the City."

"Oi'd not be going down there if Oi was ye, young Sirrah. Did ye not know there's a terrible sickness? It started off with the Elves from the tannery. They are dying in droves and they've set up a quarantine hospital care for them to try and find a cure. The City is a dangerous place. Oi'm after a bit of fresh air, meself."

Archie burst out. "But that's just why I'm here. I must find Signet. I've got some important information about the disease that's affecting Altair."

Fingal rubbed his chin thoughtfully. "It's Signet Eolzig ye'll be looking for. With information about the plague an' all, ye say. Well that's different then. Oi'd better be helping ye."

"Do you know where Signet is?"

"Well, Oi wouldn't be knowin' for certain, but Oi'd put me money on it that he'll be at the Court House, having a meeting with Asphodel and the Altairian Council. Come along now. Oi'll show ye the way."

Archie asked him, "How come you have an Irish accent?"

Fingal looked back at him quizzically. "An accent you say; Well, Oi learnt to speak the Gaelic and English when Oi made my rite of passage visit to Earth, to Ireland. It's a beautiful country, so it is. But Oi've not got an accent. Tis yerself that has the accent."

Fingal laughed and Archie couldn't help joining in. He wasn't sure if the Leprechaun was teasing him, but looking at it from Fingal's point of view certainly made him think.

"What's a rite of—"

Fingal interrupted Archie and kept up a stream of conversation so that he could hardly get a word in. He pointed out the different habitations as they passed and told Archie who lived there. Archie saw lines of cottages going back into the hills as far as the eye could see. Fingal told him that they belonged to the Flower Fairies. Archie was not surprised as the cottages were half the size of an Earth house and each had a beautiful garden which seemed to have a colour theme.

Archie craned his neck to look back as they made such a pretty sight. He saw there were one or two semi-circular structures in each garden and creatures that looked like bees were swarming around going in and out. Then he noticed a Fairy in one of the gardens who was hanging out her washing. There were Fairy dresses of all sizes—large, medium and small, and even a tiny one.

"Are there families of—"

"Now, that's where the Shining Beings live," Fingal said pointing to what seemed to be a temple up on the hills. "They are like angels so they are, and they are the same size as ye humans. They have a shimmering translucent appearance and they are shape shifters so that they can take on a particular appearance for a particular task. Sometimes they're called Devas. There are four of them, one for each of the elements. Let me see . . . Kiera is the Deva of the Air, Imrir is the Deva of Fire, and Assa is the Deva of Water. Now let me see, who have Oi missed out?"

"Earth," Archie prompted. "That's what you call Terra."

"Oh to be sure Erda is yer Earth Deva. Now you see each one is a guardian of a portal into other worlds. They have responsibility for the creatures of their particular element and they see that peace and harmony is maintained here on Altair. We haven't always had peace. There have been some bumpy patches, but the Shining Ones always manage to smooth out any troubles. See the forest over there? Well, that's where all the Gnomes live. They are the farmers and grow vegetables and kind of crops a bit like your wheat, and barley."

"What do you—"

"Will ye just look over there?" He pointed to another mountain, "Ye can just see some caves. That's where the Goblins live. They work the mines. You want to make sure ye don't go near them. They're a mean, bad tempered, spiteful crew."

As they came nearer to the city there were more and more houses all of different shapes and sizes. Fingal knew everyone who lived in each house and called out a "Jurgen Sast," or, "Ka te see," as he passed.

"What does Jurgen Sast and Ka te see mean? And how many different creatures live in Altair? And what's a rite of passage, and what do you all eat, and do you have money?" Archie blurted out all the questions that he had been trying to ask Fingal.

"Ah, well now, Jurgen Sast means Good Morning and the closest translation for Ka te see is balance or well-being. We use it for a greeting on Altair; I suppose it's like saying Oi wish you well. Now let me see . . . there are many many different tribes of people that live here on Altair, far too many to name them all. Ye see there are other lands on the planet, but this city Uckbata is the capital of all of Altair. We call it the Shining City because the Shining Beings live here. Now what else were ye after knowin'?

"Aah yes, rites of passage. Everyone who lives on Altair has to complete their rites of passage before they become a citizen of Altair, and they are allowed to vote in elections. We call it the Serai. We can go to four different planets and we have to complete a study and write it up, when we come back. We get lots of ideas from these studies and we vote whether to introduce them here. There are two planets, which are a little more advanced than us. The Altairians who go there live among its peoples, and they are accepted. Now on the other two planets where life is more primitive, like yer Earth—"

Archie gave a gasp of surprise at that but didn't want to interrupt Fingal.

"—We can't show our faces. The Earth isn't ready for the new technology we could show them. It would only lead to war and strife and there's enough of that down there already. Now the only time we can show ourselves is . . . "

Archie looked at him expectantly, thinking he was going to mention something serious.

" . . . when someone has had more than ten pints of beer, so that when he wakes up in the morning, he'll think he dreamt our meetin'."

Fingal's eyes twinkled and he gave a deep throaty chuckle. Archie joined in and understood immediately why there were so many stories of magical creatures appearing on Earth.

Fingal continued, "Oi went to Oirland as it's a tradition in our family to go there. Me father and grandfather went there before me."

Archie's head was spinning and his mind was doing somersaults.

"Oi'll tell ye more about Altair, so Oi will, as it'll take us a good ten minutes to walk to the city."*

* To read more of what Fingal told Archie about Altair see the Appendix.

Chapter Twelve

Uckbata

Fingal stopped talking as they approached the City walls. There was a large archway and a huge wooden door. Archie noticed that there were strange hieroglyphics carved on the wall. Fingal had warned him that there would be a Gillyaid guarding the gate as they were the official "policemen" of Altair. Fingal raised the enormous metal knocker and the door opened. Archie was fascinated by the Gillyaid. The top half looked like a lion with a tawny mane, then the torso was humanlike with long arms but his two legs were long and spindly like a giraffe.

"Jurgen Sast," the Gillyaid said in a deep throaty voice.

Fingal quickly replied, rattling off a stream of words in Altairian.

The Gillyaid kept glancing at Archie and then his mouth curved in a semblance of a smile and he said hesitantly, as if speaking in a foreign language, "Welcome to Uckbata. You will finding—no I should say find—Signet at the Courthouse. Fingal will take you there. Have a nice day."

Archie started to laugh because the "have a nice day" sounded like Arnold Schwarzenegger when he was in the film *The Terminator*. Fingal caught on and joined in with his hearty chuckle.

"You'll have to excuse the Gillyaid. You see they never visit Terra. They go to another planet so he only speaks a little English that he has picked up from Serraim who have visited Terra."

Archie nodded in acknowledgment but he soon forgot the Gillyaid as he was spellbound by all the different shops lining the avenue. There was a shop that seemed to be a greengrocer with all manner of strange looking fruit and vegetables. Next door there was a shop selling all shapes and sizes of metal containers. Some were jug shaped and some looked like saucepans. There were plates, cups, hammers, wrenches, saws, nails and rows of other familiar objects. He stopped dead when he noticed that all the shop signs seemed to be in English.

The greengrocers sign read "Hinkle and Sons: Purveyors of the Finest Fruit and Vegetables." The Hardware shop displayed a sign stating, "Pampertons: Suppliers of Crockery and Utensils to the Donus for the Last 50 Years."

"Why are all the shop signs in English?" Archie asked Fingal.

Fingal looked up at the sign and said in a surprised voice, "Oi didn't know it was programmed for English as well. Ye see Archie, there's a hidden camera that focuses on the person reading the sign and it recognises what type of being ye are and automatically flashes the sign into yer own language. We have three hundred different tribes living on Altair and each speaks a different language. It must've recognised that ye were a Terran. Now watch, if Oi stand and look at the sign, it'll change."

As Archie watched, the sign changed into an undecipherable jumble of words and then it began to flash between this and English.

"Wow that must be your language."

"Sure enough, that's Leprechaunese and because we're both looking at the sign. It's alternating between the two languages."

Archie kept looking back at the last shop in astonishment but then his nostrils picked up the most wonderful smell and he forgot about the sign. It was like new baked bread but somehow sweeter and more appetising. The aroma was coming from a Baker's shop and inside there were shelves full what appeared to be bread, rolls, cakes, buns, and pies. The sight and smell made Archie's mouth water.

Fingal glanced at Archie and noticed his expression. He disappeared into the shop and Archie could hear the exchange of, "Jurgen Sast," followed by a unfathomable discussion in Altairian. Fingal came out smiling with two enormous pies.

"Now, Oi could see ye were hungry so Oi've got us both a pie. Oi was feelin' a bit peckish meself. These are filled with Ugora, which we grow here, and it contains all the protein and vitamins that ye'll ever need. It's very filling so it'll stop ye feelin' hungry, sure enough."

Archie bit into the delicious looking pie. "Mmm it's yummy." He was so hungry that anything would have tasted good but this pie was indescribably scrumptious. It tasted better than anything he had ever eaten and it tasted like nothing he had ever eaten. The two of them munched happily as they sat together in companionable silence on a bench under a strange looking tree.

"Whew, I'm stuffed," Archie said as he rubbed his stomach.

"Oi told ye it would satisfy yer hunger," Fingal said laughing as he too finished his pie and relaxed back into the bench.

Now that he was no longer hungry, Archie started to feel agitated. "We'd better go. I've got to find Signet. How far is it to the Courthouse?"

"Hold on now, will ye. We can't interrupt the meeting. They'll have a mid-morning break, so they will, so we can catch him then. But if Oi know Signet, he'll know ye're here an' he'll be looking for ye, so he will."

"'It was afternoon when I left Earth. How come it's only the morning here?"

Fingal looked up at the sky "Well, time is a bit different on Altair. Will ye just look up there? You can see the morning moon and when it disappears from sight, it's about mid morning here on Altair. Ye can see that the morning moon is just about to set and so we've got a bit of time, so we have. Oi'll tell ye what. Oi'm a bit thirsty and ye must be thirsty too, so we'll stop for a drink at that café over there where can see the Courthouse. We'll see all the Big Nobs come out of their meeting. We'll be able to catch Signet then."

Chapter Thirteen

The Schlock Shop

As they made their way along the main street towards the square and the café, Archie noticed a large shop and the sign displayed read, "The Schlock Shop." Under the sign it said, "Dealers in Odd Socks" and under this it said, "Recycled and New Clothing at Reasonable Prices." There was a colourful display of suits, trousers, dresses, jumpers, shirts and T shirts clothes in the windows and on rails outside.

Archie was fascinated. "What's that?" he asked Fingal.

"Ah, that'd be a clothes shop. It's run by two Mizakeen, Lev and Soli; they're shape shifters you know." Noticing Archie's puzzled expression he continued. "Have ye never heard of shape shifters? Well they can change their shape to whatever form they want. Usually they change to their customer's shape, I suppose the customers feel more comfortable and Lev and Soli make more sales."

"But why are they dealers in odd socks?"

"Well now, that's how they got started. They're mischievous by nature and when they went to Terra on their Serai, they used to take one sock from a pair, just to tease people. They brought back a pile of single socks and started their business by unpicking the wool or the cotton fibres and dying them and make pairs of socks, coats, suits and all sorts of clothes. Now it's become a tradition with the Mizakeen that when they visit Terra they take single socks and bring back piles of these for Lev and Sol."

54

Archie started to laugh. "So that's why my Mum complains that we always end up with odd socks. She says one sock disappears, like magic, off the face of the Earth."

Fingal laughed again. "She's right! They've been sent to Lev and Soli's Schlock Shop on Altair."

"Why is it called The Schlock shop?"

"It's a play on words, you see Schlock means cheap tat, rubbish in Yiddish, you see the Mizakeen always do their Serai in Jewish families, so they pick up Yiddish on Terra. But they don't just trade in socks now. No, when they became more successful they branched out and they recycle many different fabrics from the four planets we visit. They're very clever businessmen. Here you are now; they must've heard us talking, so you can meet them yourself. "

Archie looked at the shop and saw a flash and two men appeared.

"Look, Soli, socks!" one exclaimed looking at Archie's socks.

"Didn't I tell you they'd come back in fashion." He smiled at Archie and beckoned to him. "Come in, my boy, have we got socks for you. We got knee high socks, ankle socks, trainer socks, sports socks, bed socks, thermal socks, wool socks, cotton socks, acrylic socks, even cashmere socks, patterned socks, plain socks, argyle socks, striped socks, spotted socks and even tartan socks. We got black socks, white socks, red socks, blue socks, yellow socks, orange socks, purple socks and even sky blue pink socks. Fluffy socks, smooth socks. You want socks, my boy? We got socks. Boy, have you come to the right place."

The man had said all this without drawing a breath and Archie looked at him in astonishment.

The other man put his hand on the others arm as if to restrain him. "Alright, Lev, Don't confuse the boy. Come in and we'll give you a glass of Velvberry juice. You could probably use it after listening to my friend here. Fingal, my old friend, I know you're partial to Irish Whisky. Our nephew is on Serai and he sent it, so you can tell us if it's any good. "

The inside of the shop was cool and dark after the bright sunlight, and as Archie's eyes adjusted, he could see vast rails and shelves of clothes arranged neatly, each area displaying signs. He looked around and noticed that the signs seemed to be in alphabetical order like a Library. He read "Abatwa, Ballybogs, Bean Nighe, Sidhe and Tighe, Blue men, Bogarts, Bokwas, Brownies, Blue hags, and Cluicaun." He got no further than that as Lev handed him a glass containing a liquid the colour of bright turquoise.

"Enjoy," he said as he poured Fingal a large glass of whiskey.

Both Lev and Soli had a glass of the turquoise juice and they raised them and said, "Mazel Tov."

Archie hesitated for a moment as the juice was such a peculiar colour, but he was thirsty and he took a small sip to see if he liked it. It was the most refreshing fruity taste and certainly nothing like he had expected or had ever tasted before. He liked it so much that he gulped the juice down without stopping and Lev refilled his glass. The drink was thirst quenching and he sipped the second glass while Fingal told Lev and Soli about his mission.

They were both nodding thoughtfully and Soli announced that he would come with them to find Signet while Lev managed the shop.

"We might be able to help as we have lots of connections with doctors, medicine and hospitals on Planet Earth."

Archie was curious and asked, "Why is that?"

Lev answered, "We are Mizakeen and traditionally we always visit the Jewish people on Terra. Many of our peoples become doctors on Altair, you see, and so when they do their Serai, naturally they go to observe hospitals, doctors and medical research centres to learn the latest medical advances."

"Aah, is that why you've written all the display signs in the shop in English?

"That's right, my boy. Most people know where their section is, but this system helps us in the running of the shop and we can point people in the right direction if they need help."

Archie explored the shop while Fingal chatted to Lev and Soli. He was attracted to a shirt that was hanging up with a sign saying, "New material, Dirt resistant. Never needs washing! Thermally balanced to adjust to temperature. Cools you in the heat and warms you up when you are cold!" It looked grey from a distance, but up close Archie could see it had a small black check. Archie examined the shirt and touched it. The material felt like very fine cotton and had a sheen to it. It looked like a Ralph Lauren or Yves St Laurent. In fact, it was just the sort of shirt Archie loved.

Lev noticed that Archie kept coming back to the shirt. "Ah you have good taste, my boy. It's the latest material. The Gillyaids brought it back from the planet Zima in the constellation of Rigel, one of the advanced planets we visit. The Council have agreed to let us use it on Altair. You never need to wash it as it repels dirt, and if you get a stain on it, it will remove the stain gradually over a short time. It adjusts to your temperature so it cools you down when you're hot and warms you up when you're cold."

Archie took the shirt down from the stand and held it up against him.

"Try it on my boy; it looks about your size."

Archie didn't need any further persuasion and put the shirt on over his T shirt.

"Will you come and see this, Soli, Fingal. It's perfect. Do you look good or what, my boy? Come and see, Soli."

Fingal turned round to look. "Ah, ye look as beautiful as an angel, so ye do. You would outshine one of the Shining Beings."

Archie looked at himself in the mirror and liked what he saw. "How much is it?" he asked.

"It's a lot of credits. Twenty credits to be exact."

"What are credits? Is that your money?"

"Yes, that's right."

"Oh I see," Archie said in a crestfallen voice. "I don't have any credits."

Soli came up to Archie. "I tell you what we do. For you, my

boy, I can see you like the shirt so we'll exchange it for your socks. I know your socks aren't worth 20 credits, but we can recycle them and we'll count the rest as a gift."

Archie didn't waste a second; He took off his socks and handed them to Soli. He didn't care that they were his favourite ones; he just wanted the shirt. "Cool! thanks. Soli, I really appreciate it."

Soli smiled at his enthusiasm, "Come on then, we'd better go and see if the Council has come out yet. Will you be alright on your own for a while, Lev?"

"Go on. I can manage, but come back and tell me the news or I'll die of curiosity."

Fingal's eyes twinkled and he winked at Archie as he called back to Lev. "Well don't shift your shape to a cat."

"Why?" Lev asked.

"Curiosity killed the cat, don't you know!"

Everybody laughed, including Lev and they could still hear him chortling as they walked towards the Courthouse.

Chapter Fourteen

The High Council of Altair

As the three of them approached the steps leading to the Council Building, Archie looked at the massive structure in awe. It was white and it seemed to shimmer in the sunlight. He guessed that it was painted with the same Lumenite paint that had been used in the Oosha. The steps stretched across the whole width of the building and there were pillars all along the front, which made it look like pictures he had seen of the Parthenon in Athens. The wooden doors were even larger than the ones at the entrance of the Oosha. Archie had no further time to study the Council Building as Signet appeared in his flowing white robes through the grand looking doors and called out a greeting.

"Ka te see, Fingal. Ka te see, Soli. Welcome to Altair, Archie. I knew you were here and I worked out that you must have discovered something important about the plague on Altair. This epidemic is baffling all the doctors here. I was about to go back to Terra, but when I felt you arrive I waited for you. The Council thinks that someone has brought this dread disease back to Altair from one of the four planets they visit. They have summoned the Altairians who supervise the Seraim and ordered them to go back and investigate. As I look after the Seraim on Earth, I was about to go back to Terra, but when I felt you arrive, I waited for you."

Archie told him everything about the time when he and his

sister had seen Vastator. He also told him that they had overheard the plans for a bank robbery and how they planned to snatch the Faberge eggs at the Marina and hand it in to the Security guards.

Signet kept nodding. He was worried but tried not to show it. "Thank you, Archie, that's very helpful and it narrows down the diagnosis of the epidemic. We now know it's coming from Earth. Well, well, well, Vastator, my old enemy again. I thought we had seen the last of him for a few more years."

Signet was troubled. He thought back to the last time that they had all faced the evil Vastator. Ally had showed him such kindness that he was banished by her actions back into the abyss. Vastator's only weakness was if someone showed kindness to him. It was the only way he could be overcome, for then his bright time on Earth ended and he was swallowed into a deep dark sleep. This was the only time Signet had witnessed the effect of kindness on Vastator and he had rather hoped his banishment would be permanent. He wasn't frightened of Vastator. He had met plenty of evil entities over the years, and none of them had yet got the better of him.

But this new information meant that the disease had come from Terra and, since it came from Vastator in particular, that meant the situation was dangerous. He knew that he was always trying to lengthen his stay on Earth by creating evil. Signet felt guilty. He was supposed to keep an eye on all the Seraim on Terra and he knew that Vastator must have charmed or tricked one of them into helping him. Signet knew that Vastator had not visited Altair because he would have sensed his evil emanations. So if Vastator was behind this, he must therefore be aware of the existence of Altair.

Signet wondered how he had failed. He thought in his own defence that he was always busy. He guarded all the sacred places on Earth where ley lines crossed, and he supervised the Seraim. But still, he felt it was his fault and he cursed himself silently. Then there was magic, the ancient art. It was so important to pass on the knowledge. Otherwise it would be lost and forgotten, a wispy spider web swept away with a laugh as nonsense. It was dismissed by unbelievers as fantasy and foolishness, dreamed of by hopefuls longing for the lost art, and for most just 'a once upon a time' myth. He had to make sure that whoever he chose was worthy. He had been grooming Archie and setting him a series of tests that, so far, he had passed. But all this took up his time, and he worried that his attention had strayed.

He thought about Vastator. Vastator did not have any personal animus against the human race, but if it came to a conflict between their feelings and his continued existence, there could be no choice. It was this fact had made Vastator such a treacherous and dangerous entity. Signet wondered how he would feel if he were in the same position. It must be incredibly frustrating that the reactions of 'mere humans' dictated his life. Signet thought that given Vastator's dilemma, he would just go back into the cold blackness to save the world from more evil. Did this mean that Vastator was intrinsically wicked, or did it mean that he was wrong and that anyone in Vastator's position, including him would react in the same way? It was a conundrum that he could not solve and it did not help him in this present crisis.

Archie, Soli and Fingal watched Signet as he mused. Archie was keen to go in to the Council Building and he tugged Signet's sleeve.

"Shall we go in now?"

"Ooh, I'm so sorry, I was immersed in my own thoughts that I quite forgot about you all for a moment. Come. We'll go in now."

They walked up the massive steps between the giant pillars and Signet ushered them through the door.

Archie found himself in a large hall and as he looked around, he thought the inside was just as awesome as the outside. The hall was high and there was a staircase leading upwards that split and divided into two staircases at either side. It had no windows but it was very light and Archie noticed that there were lights that looked familiar to him. These were definitely Lumenite.

"We're in the smaller upper meeting room," Signet said as he led the way up the stairs. The three followed in silence as he took the left-hand stairway and finally showed them into a large room.

Archie could hardly stop himself from saying, "Wow," but he thought, "No way is this small."

There was a long table, which ran for the whole length of the room, and sitting round it were the strangest collection of people he had ever seen. He recognised some of them from pictures in fairy tale books, but most were creatures or beings that he had never seen before. Some were sitting on chairs but others were sitting on other contraptions, obviously designed to suit their physical forms.

At the top of the table there was another table on a raised dais placed at right angles to the long table, making the shape of the letter T. There was a Unicorn sitting on its haunches at the centre of the table, and two people that looked like angels were sitting on each side of her. They had wings and seemed to shine and glow with a kind of inner light. Archie knew that they were the four Elementals or Shining Beings that Fingal had told him about.

There were some spaces at the top of the table and Signet guided them to these spaces, which had obviously been made for them. With a sweep of his hand, he made the introductions, "Asphodel, Kiera, Imrir, Assa, Erda and Learned Elders, this is Archie, Fingal and Soli. Archie, Fingal and Soli this is Asphodel, the Elementals and all the Learned Elders."

Everybody smiled and nodded at the three newcomers. Archie felt comfortable and at ease and he took the offered seat.

Fingal sat down next to him and turned on a small monitor on the table in front of Archie. "This is for those who don't speak Altairian. It'll translate what's being said into your own language." He pressed the screen as commands popped up in bubbles on the screen.

"Cool," Archie said as he noticed that they did not use a mouse, as he did on his own computer, back home on earth. Each time a person spoke; a bubble appeared on the screen. He pressed it and found to his delight that as well as translating what they were saying, it came up with the person's name and tribe. It saved him from whispering questions to Fingal about who they all were, which might have appeared rude.

Signet moved to a small raised platform on the right-hand side and addressed the top table and the council in Altairian. Archie followed the translation on his screen.

"As you know, Archie has brought some important information for us from Terra," Signet announced and he repeated Archie's suspicions about the Terran origins of the disease. He did not mention Vastator at this stage because he felt that to do so might panic the entire Council. There were several gasps, and when Signet had finished, the meeting disrupted into mayhem. Everybody stood up, waved their hands about and shouted at once.

Asphodel called the meeting to order by using her hoof as a gavel and said, "Enough."

There was complete silence and you could have heard a pin drop.

"One at a time,"

Everyone sat down and the calm peaceful atmosphere returned.

"Gretorix, as the epidemic started with the Elves, you may speak first."

The Elf stood up and addressed the meeting, "Why would any Terran want to kill the Elven tribe? We've never done them any harm. If we can find the answer, we can stop the epidemic."

"Sashika?"

Archie watched as a fairy stood up and began to speak. If he had seen her in the street in his hometown, he would have said, "Wow, she's a sort," but somehow it seemed disrespectful to even think this on Altair.

"I don't think knowing the answer to these questions will help. We need to know what this disease *is* before it spreads throughout Altair."

Archie heard several comments which he thought comments

like agreement and these were confirmed on his communicator monitor when he read, "Hear, hear," and, "Well said."

"Souhei?"

A magnificent golden fox started to speak in a deep gravely voice. Archie was amazed as he looked like a fox but he had five tails.. . He saw on his communicator screen that he was a Kitsune.

"Tell us the symptoms again, Gretorix, because now that we know this disease is from Terra, we will be able to identify it."

The Elf stood up, "Fever, headache, sore throat, weakness, nausea, constipation, shortness of breath and sometimes it seems to develop into pneumonia."

Souhei spoke again "I sense that Signet has the key to the problem.."

Archie watched Signet as he banged his hand on his head, as if he had just thought of something. He began to pace up and down between the top and the bottom tables.

"Do the victims ever have large lumps like a swollen lymph gland anywhere on their body? It swells up like a ball? " Signet asked the Elf.

"Ah, yes, I'd forgotten that."

"I have it. I have the answer. Bubonic plague. I've seen it before. I saw it in the fifth and sixth centuries in the Mediterranean region, in 14th Century Europe, and in 1855 in China. It's deadly. The rat flea spreads it. The infected rats carry the plague and transmit it to fleas living on their bodies. The organism is transmitted to people by being bitten by these fleas. Someone must be putting the fleas on the rats and bringing them to Altair. We have to stop it or we'll have a pandemic. Have you found any dead rats or giant mice, as you call them?"

Several people around the table made noises of consternation. Archie saw the comments translated on his communicator,

"What are we to do?"

"I've never known anything like this."

"We must act quickly."

Soli stood up. "I think I can help. My father wrote a paper on new Terran medical developments back when he was on Serai. I remember there was some reference to the use of what Terran people describe as antibiotics to cure previously untreatable Terran diseases like the plague. Our physicians are enormously sophisticated dealing as they do, with three hundred different life forms and they have developed ways of improving our immune systems. We are protected against all the Altairian diseases, but we are not protected against Terran diseases. Our immune systems cannot cope with this infection, and so we'll have to find the antibiotics on Terra and bring them back."

"Thank you, Soli." Asphodel acknowledged the Mizakeen's contribution.

The Elemental called Erda spoke, "Whoever is behind this must be using one of our people to bring the infected creatures to Altair. We have to find out how this infection got into Altair and how it evaded the vigilance of the Ministry of Learning."

Asphodel held up her hoof as a storm of angry voices broke out. "The Shining Beings and I will retire for a short break to discuss what is to be done. Please remain seated and we will return to give you our decision."

A voice rang out, "All rise," and all the people around the table stood up while Asphodel and the four Devas disappeared through a door in the wall behind the platform.

After a very short period, the Councillors rose to their feet as Asphodel and the four Devas re-entered the hall. When they were all seated, Asphodel spoke calmly but strongly to a hushed audience.

"It is clear that our planet faces a great danger. At present, we are not sure who is the cause of this threat and why. We do not know whether it is accidental or by design. We believe the disease emanates from beyond Altair but do not yet know how to combat it. Most importantly, we do not know how much time we have to fight this menace before it overwhelms us all.

"We propose the formation of a Special Task Force, whose remit will be to answer all the questions I have posed but cannot presently answer. This Special Task Force will comprise members from the Ministry of Medicine, the Ministry of Learning, together with Gretorix, chief of the Elven tribe, the Elven Seraim Master and Signet, our Terran Ambassador. They have two Altairian days to present their initial report, and they will have all our resources behind them. They may call whatever witnesses and evidence they require. All Altair's hopes rest with them. Let this meeting adjourn and the Task Force's initial works begin. There is no time to lose.

Chapter Fifteen

The Special Task Force

Archie watched as everyone filed out of the hall. Soon there was just Signet, Soli, Fingal and Gretorix the chief of the Elven tribe.

Signet said, "Asphodel will summon three members from the Ministry of Medicine and three from the Ministry of Learning. I expect they'll be here soon so you'd better contact your Seraim Master." He nodded to Gretorix.

Gretorix used his Theolite communicator. "Hello, Pauntil, Gretorix here. Can you come to the Council Building immediately? Asphodel and the Devas have appointed a Special Task Force to solve the problem of the epidemic and she has co-opted you on to it." He listened for a few moments and said, "Okay. We'll expect you in a few minutes then."

Fingal stood up. "Oi'll wait outside for ye, Archie. Oi expect you'll be returning to Terra, so Oi'll want to say good bye."

Just as Fingal went out of the door, there was a humming noise and three shapes shimmered into solid people.

Signet said, "Welcome to the Special Task Force, I'm afraid I don't know your names and so you'll have to introduce yourselves."

A tall dark-haired attractive woman with beautiful blue eyes stepped forward. "I'm Doctor Beshley from the Bean Tighe tribe and I am in charge of the contagious disease department at the Ministry of Medicine."

A baboon-like man, who was covered with long back fur, introduced himself. "I'm Doctor Kiddush of the Tokolyush tribe. I am the Head of Virology at the Ministry of Medicine."

The third person stepped forward and he was the most spectacular as he wore war paint on his face. "I'm Doctor Hokusain and I'm from the tribe of Bokwus. I'm head of the Department of Epidemiology, the study of epidemics, at the Ministry of Medicine."

Signet introduced the others to the newcomers, just as another shape materialised into an Elf.

Gretorix stepped forward, and said, "This is Pauntil, the Seraim Master for the Elven tribe." He introduced him to all the others and they all took seats on the main table waiting for the three representatives from Ministry of Learning to arrive.

Archie was fascinated at how these beings just materialised and kept looking around the room, wondering where the next person would emerge. He did not have long to wait as there was a humming sound and the air seemed to vibrate just behind him. He swivelled round in his chair and three shapes became visible right in front of his eyes.

"I am Colonel Gurin from the Gillyaid tribe. I am in charge of the Office for the Protection of Altair. We screen all data, products and new technology and people before allowing them into Altair." He looked directly at Archie and said with a chuckle, "It's all right, young Archie. Signet has already cleared your arrival with our Security Division."

A small winged creature stepped forward. "I'm Professor Santha from the Sylph tribe and I'm in charge of Terra Seraim projects."

The third person was a bird and Archie could not help staring, as it seemed to be a mixture of birds he knew from Earth. The head was like a golden pheasant and the body duck-like with an amazing peacock tail. It had long legs, a beak like a parrot and swallow wings. The bird spoke "I am Yin Zheng of the Fenghuang. I'm in charge of order and harmony on Altair and report directly to the Divas."

Signet once again introduced all the new arrivals and when everyone was seated he began. "As you all know, we are here to investigate and find the source and the cure for this disease that is spreading rapidly among the Altairians. Firstly, we should elect a Chairman."

"I propose Signet," Gretorix said.

"I second that," Colonel Gurin boomed out in his deep voice.

Signet held up his hand. "I cannot accept the Chair. I am not an Altairian and I have other responsibilities. I could be called back to Terra at any time. It would be better if someone else was elected."

There was a silence for a moment while everyone looked around at each other, wondering who would make the best chairman.

Signet broke the silence. "I propose Gretorix of the Elven tribe as his people are the ones who have been the victims of this disease, so far."

Doctor Hokusain immediately replied, "I second that."

Signet looked around the table. "Are there any objections? No? Well in that case, Gretorix is our Chairman and will start the proceedings."

He leaned over and whispered something to Gretorix, who nodded and began to speak, "Before we agree on the tasks that each person will undertake, my friend Signet would like to address you."

"I am the custodian of several sacred or special Terran sites. I am not alone as an immortal on Terra. There is one semi-eternal entity that I have crossed swords with on many occasions. This entity is called into being by evil and malice. He disappears for an indeterminate period only to be recalled when a further outbreak of evil occurs. His name is Vastator. I have not talked about Vastator before because he exists only on Terra and knows nothing of life on other planets. I mention him now, as I know that he is aware of and has an interest in Altair.

"Indeed, I suspect he is behind this epidemic on Altair. His interest is a major threat to the security of the tribes of Altair. One of the reasons I have for refusing the Chair of this Task Force is that I may be called back to Terra at any time to deal with Vastator. I hope, but don't know for sure, that his evil powers are just restricted to Terra. One of the aims of this group is to find out more about Vastator's intentions and to thwart them *before* he gets any chance of reaching Altair and causing mayhem."

"Thank you, Signet. That's fine, I agree, but I think it is more important to find a cure for this disease and so I think that Soli should return to Terra with Archie as soon as possible to obtain supplies of the antibiotics that he thinks might cure this disease. If this proves to be the case, it will solve our immediate problem until we can reproduce our own supplies in our laboratories. Do you all agree? Yes, Doctor Beshley?"

"How does Soli know that this medicine will work, and how does he know the name of it and where to find it?"

"Soli?" Gretorix gestured to him to stand up and speak.

"I will look up the name of the antibiotics in my father's Serai study. They are all kept in the Library. There is no reason to suppose that they will not work on us as they cure the Plague in humans. I know they keep supplies in pharmacies in hospitals, so I'll use my Theolite to make myself invisible and collect as much as I can carry back with me."

Doctor Kiddush stood up. "If we know the name and the composition of the drug, wouldn't it be better to make it here in our laboratories?"

Doctor Hokusain spoke, "We thought about that as a solution, but we are not sure that we can get it exactly right, whether it will be suitable for our different Altairian life forms or how long it will take to produce. When we have the answers to these questions, we will be able to reproduce our own drug in a matter of hours."

Gretorix stood up. "So do we all agree that Soli should be given the task of bringing back the trial antibiotics to Altair?"

There were noises of assent from everyone.

"The proposal is carried unanimously. Soli will go back to Terra immediately with Archie, and will return as quickly as possible with the antibiotics."

"Signet?"

"I will be in charge of all the investigations on Terra and if Vastator has any evil plans that involve Altair, I *will* stop him. I have the power to travel back in time and so I propose to go back a few weeks to see what evidence I can find of Vastator's involvement."

Doctor Beshley stood up. "In the meantime, I will be in charge of the quarantine arrangements. We have made Uckbata a no-go area. No one is to be allowed to travel in or out of the City. We will be putting out bulletins to advise people of the symptoms of the disease. We have issued instructions to all the different tribes around Uckbata to stay in their homes until further notice."

Doctor Kiddush stood up as Doctor Beshley sat down. "I will be in charge of collecting samples of the virus and growing cultures so that we can study it and experiment on ways of killing the virus. We will be comparing these with other known viruses on our database."

Doctor Hokusain took over. "My department will be studying past patterns of the spreading of this disease so that when we have further information about how to combat the virus, we will be able to predict the speed, method and extent of the outbreak. We will also be looking at our tribes' differing physiologies to predict which will be susceptible to the virus."

Gretorix spoke, "Thank you. Now, the Ministry of Learning, what are your plans?"

Colonel Gurin stood up and in his deep booming voice said, "We will be responsible for policing the curfew in Uckbata and make sure that people stay in their homes. We will also make sure that we maintain security surrounding the City so that, as far as possible, we will stop anyone from leaving or, indeed, anyone from entering."

"Fine. Professor Santha?"

"I will be studying all the reports received from Seraim for the last two years to see if someone has brought anything relevant to this disease back from one of the planets. I know we believe that it has come from Terra, but if two different 'off Altair' imports could possibly have combined in some way to create this present situation, we need to know. There is a slim chance, but we must check it out."

Yin Zheng fluffed out her wings and said. "We will be studying how different societies on Terra have dealt with past epidemics to see if there is anything we can learn from Terra about how to handle this situation here. My partner Yang Rong of the Earth dragons will be helping me."

Gretorix nodded and turned to the Seraim master for the Elven tribe. "Pauntil?"

"I have several Seraim on Terra at the moment and I will send them all a message to let them know of the situation back here. I will ask them to send a report back immediately to let us know if anyone suspicious has approached them, asking questions about Altair and maybe given them something to bring back to Altair."

Signet stood up. "Don't mention the situation on Altair. Just ask them to send an interim report and ask if they have made any Terran friends. If Vastator is behind this epidemic, I don't want anyone to alert him. He's a maverick and you never know what he might do if he thinks his plans have been discovered."

Pauntil replied slowly as he was thinking while he spoke, "Yes, I see what you mean. I won't mention the epidemic, but I'll send them a questionnaire that will provide the information we need without ringing any alarm bells for any Terran they may be helping."

Signet nodded his thanks and Gretorix spoke, "Well, that all seems fine. Is there any aspect that we have left uncovered?"

Everyone shook their heads and Gretorix carried on. "Good. We will meet back here when the evening moon has risen.

Asphodel has put this room at our disposal and if you need to contact me with any urgent information I will be here. Good luck, everyone."

Chapter Sixteen

Return to Terra

Doctor Beshley materialised in the reception area of the quarantine ward. Fresh from the meeting of the Special Task Force, she knew she had a lot to do. Her first task was to find everyone new clothes to wear and collect and incinerate their old clothes. It was necessary because rat fleas had spread this disease that had come from Terra, and they had probably contaminated the hospital already. She found some of her team of volunteers and sent them off to the laundry to bring back all the hospital orderlies and surgeons outfits they could find. She had her communicator in her hand and was just about to make a call when she heard someone calling her name. She looked up and saw Thorin, the owner of the tannery, running towards her.

"Doctor Beshley, Doctor Beshley, I'm so glad I found you. My son Zegar is sick and I'm so worried about him. He seems to be getting worse very quickly. One minute he was fine and the next he was hot and feverish and complaining about a sore throat."

The Doctor looked at Thorin. She did not want to say that any illness developed far speedier in the young, but instead she wanted to give him hope. She chose her words carefully and said, "We know it's a disease that has come from Terra, and Soli, the Mizakeen is going back to Terra with a young Terran named Archie to get some drugs that will cure the disease. Archie is a friend of Signet's and he came to bring us this information. I promise you that as soon as they come back, your son will be the first to be given the drug."

She did not know that Thorin had a nephew Julian carrying out his Serai on Terra and so she did not think it was necessary to give him a warning to keep this information secret.

Thorin nodded. "Thank you, Doctor Beshley."

"I'll come and look at Zegar in a moment. There is one thing you can do, give his clothes to the nurse. We are destroying everything that you Elves were wearing as a precaution to stop the disease spreading. We will be distributing other clothes for you to wear."

Thorin went back to the ward and sat next to his wife by Zegar's bed. He anxiously watched his son for some sign of improvement. He seemed to be getting worse by the minute. He was burning hot and delirious with fever. He looked so small and vulnerable in the hospital bed. Thorin could hardly bear to watch his son's suffering as it made him feel so helpless. Then an idea came to him. He would call his nephew Julektar on Terra and tell him that Soli and Archie were going back to Terra to find the drugs they needed. He would entreat him to go and meet Soli and Archie to help them to find the drugs. Perhaps he could even bring a small amount back before they brought the whole supply. They could give these to Zegar and help to save his life.

Back in Town Hall, Signet beckoned to Soli and Archie to follow him as he went through the door behind the dais. Archie was trying to work out in Earth time when the meeting that they had talked about was going to take place. He decided that in *his* time, they meant tomorrow evening. He was constantly bombarded with new information and his mind was turning somersaults and cartwheels.

He hardly noticed the room they had entered or Soli setting off to the Library until Signet pulled out a chair for him to sit on. The room was beautiful with marble floors and pillars on two sides. Archie guessed that the Altairians must have a form of air conditioning, as the temperature was exactly right. A jug of juice and some glasses appeared, as if by magic, and Signet poured two drinks, one for himself, and one for Archie. Archie was so thirsty that he did not stop drinking until he had drained the glass.

"Aah!" He gave a gasp of satisfaction. "That was lovely."

Just at that moment Asphodel entered the room from an adjoining door and addressed Archie, "We have decided that we will give you a TAM as a backup in case something happens to Soli. Signet will show you how it works, but you are only to use it as a last resort. A piece of Theolite will be loaned to you. She smiled at Archie. "We know what fun you could have with it, but it would be bound to come to someone's notice, and Earth isn't ready for the advanced technology. We will also give you a Theolite Communicator, into which you must first enter your name and tribe. You will then be able to be in voice communication with anyone on Altair. We will disguise this as a common Terran object, like a Game Boy, so that no one will be suspicious on Terra. We trust you to guard this rock and the Communicator. You can return the rock to Signet on Altair."

Signet took Archie to one side and handed him the three items one by one. Firstly, he handed him the Theolite communicator and showed him how it worked. Next, he handed Archie the TAM; it was in a case and Archie thought it looked like a mobile phone, although he knew it had much greater powers.

"Now you can use the TAM to travel around on Earth," Signet said and went on to explain how he had to be outside and not near to any houses or trees, and he showed him how to use it and change the co-ordinates. Lastly, he handed him a piece of Theolite and said, "It's a little like the skimming stone. In fact, the skimming stone is made of Theolite and another mineral so it's not as powerful. That's why I had to touch it with my ring to make it effective. If you hold the Theolite in front of you, it makes a force field so that others will not be able to see you."

"Wow! I'll be invisible. That's cool." Archie's eyes lit up thinking of all the fun he could have if he was invisible.

"Now, I've set the co-ordinates on the TAM to take you back to Earth. You will re-materialise in the Oosha at about eight o'clock on Earth, so you'll be in time to intercept the robbery on Saturday *and* help the girls to hand the stolen Faberge eggs to the Security at the Marina. One last thing: be very careful of Vastator. He's a cunning sly devil, as well you know."

Soli came bursting through the door. "I've made a note of the antibiotics I think we need on my Communicator, so we're all set to go now."

Aloric had heard that Archie was at the Council Building and rushed through the door a minute after Soli. "Ka te see, Archie, I'm glad you're still here as I wanted to see you again."

Archie said, "Ka te see, Aloric. It's good to see you. I hope we'll be successful and Soli will bring back the antibiotics so that the plague is wiped out."

"Thank you, Archie. That is what we all hope."

Asphodel led the way outside and motioned Archie to take two steps on to a small platform. She pressed her nose against Archie's stomach and gave the Altairian greeting, "Ka te see," which seemed to serve as a goodbye as well as a greeting.

Aloric came forward and held up his hoof to Archie. Archie took hold of it and shook it, as if it was a hand. He let go and Aloric pressed his nose against his stomach.

Fingal said, "Good to meet ye, Archie, and Oi'll look forward to ye paying us a visit soon, so Oi will."

Archie held out his hand to shake the Leprechaun's and said, "Thanks for being such a good friend and showing me the way to Uckbata."

Fingal rubbed his eyes before taking Archie's hand in both of his. "Think nothin' of it. Sure an' now Oi've got a fly in me eye, silly old fool that Oi am." He quickly withdrew his hands and rubbed his eyes again.

Signet gave Archie a hug. Asphodel and Aloric tossed their heads, so that their gleaming horns looked as if they were waving. Soli took his hand and held up his own TAM.

Archie felt a sad emptiness at leaving Altair and parting from all his new friends. It was the sort of place that grabbed you so that you felt you never wanted to leave. Archie had mixed feelings as he once again experienced the kaleidoscope effect of hurtling through space back to Earth. He was looking forward to going home, but this was tinged with regret and by a strange sense of loss.

Chapter Seventeen

Vastator's Strategy

Vastator had arranged to meet his new friend Julian in the students' bar at the university. He was meeting him every other day supposedly to help him with his studies, but this was just a ploy. In reality, Vastator had a secret agenda. Any day now he expected him to receive the news that there was mysterious epidemic on Altair that was affecting many of it's Inhabitants. Of course, Vastator already knew this as he had engineered the introduction of the plague to Altair. Vastator was comfortable and sat sipping his beer. His thoughts went back over the past few weeks, basking in his own success and the certain knowledge that all his dreams were about to come true.

Everything had just fallen into place. Julian had told him about his family business, a shoe making factory and tannery. Vastator was more than interested when he mentioned one day that the beam house and tanning yard were being overrun by Grilks who were harming the Elven leather industry. When he had questioned Julian about this, it had just got better and better. He had told him that the tanning agent used on Altair was vegetable tannin extracted from the bark of the Tarran tree. The Grilks were small omnivorous rodents who ate vegetation, insects and smaller animals and had developed a taste for this bark. They had been coming across from a neighbour's farm where they usually feasted on small animals and the corn the farmers grew. The population of Grilks had grown so much that they had spread to the tannery and were becoming a nuisance.

Vastator had told Julian casually about a creature that lived on Earth that could solve the problem for the Elves. He told him that it was a carnivore rodent that preyed upon smaller rodents and that it would wipe out the Grilks. He called it a Maxi-mouse. He did not tell Julian that the Maxi-mice were, in reality, rats and that he would infest them with plague ridden fleas brought back from Kosovo and use them to introduce the Black Death to Altair. He had nonchalantly mentioned to Julian that he knew where he could find these Maxi-mice to take to Altair.

Julian's face had been a picture. His expression had been of shock-horror mixed with earnestness as he told Vastator that he would have to go to the Ministry of Learning for them to approve the use of the Maxi-mice. He had explained that any new process, technology, medicine, material or animal had to have their approval before it could be brought back to Altair.

Vastator just had not been able to help himself when he saw Julian's reaction; he had rocked back on his chair and laughed. He should have been scowling, he had thought to himself, but instead he had sympathised with the Elf about the Ministry with its bureaucratic red tape. He had commiserated with Julian that while the Ministry was considering the solution offered, the Elves' industry and livelihood were being ruined. Time did not mean anything to Vastator and consequently he could afford to be patient. Wisely, he had not tried to persuade or put any pressure on the Elf to take the Maxi-mice to Altair.

It had been Julian who had brought up the subject of the Grilks again when they next met, and he had asked Vastator if he really thought the Maxi-mice could destroy the pests, once and for all. Vastator had hardly been able to contain his excitement when Julian had shown the first signs of taking the bait. He had thrown in another little gem and told Julian that these Maxi-mice had a very short life span. After they had exterminated the Gilks, they would all die and then no one on Altair would ever know that they had been there.

Vastator had held his breath as he could see that Julian had been torn between loyalty to his tribe and to his planet. He had nearly shouted with joy when Julian had said he would take some of these creatures back to Altair as an experiment, and if it worked, he could then apply to the Ministry of Learning for a licence to import them. Julian had returned to Altair for a short break, a few weeks ago and had taken back some Maxi-mice. He had reported back to Vastator that he had successfully set them free in the Tannery.

Vastator had been playing a waiting game. As soon as he received the news from Julian that there was a plague that was spreading in Altair, he would be ready to put the next stage of his scheme into operation, a step nearer his Grail. He would sympathise with the Elf and tell him that he recognised the disease and that he knew what would cure the illness. He would explain that he could get a supply of drugs and ask Julian to take him to Altair so that he could be proclaimed a hero and be given the rock Theolite as his reward. However, Vastator's scheming was not to go as smoothly as he had planned, and some new developments would give him cause for concern.

His thoughts were interrupted when he saw Julian and he waved to him. He noticed that his face was ashen and when he reached the table and he slumped heavily into a chair.

"What's up?" Vastator asked concernedly.

"I've just spoken with my uncle in Altair. He says that there is a great sickness on the planet. All the Elves are in quarantine at the hospital. He told me that my cousin Zegar has just become sick. He says that a Terran boy called Archie is coming back with Soli, a Mizakeen, to obtain the vital drugs that will cure this disease. They are arriving any minute now in the Oosha. My uncle begged me to go and meet him to see if I can help in any way. He's desperate about his son and he thinks that my help might hurry things up. I must go straightaway. It would be terrible if anything happened to Zegar. It's a matter of life and death. The quicker we can get these antibiotics back to Altair, the better Zegar's chances are."

Vastator was so enraged that he could hardly control his temper. He brought his fist down on the table and Julian looked at him in surprise. He had not expected this distinguished professor to react so strongly, but he was pleased that he cared enough about him and his planet to be angry.

Vastator thought to himself, *that troublesome boy again. How was it that he always appeared at the wrong time and ruined everything?* He'd like to wring his neck if he could get hold of him. But there was just one chance of saving the whole strategy he had planned. If he could get just get to the Oosha in time.

Masking his anger he said to Julian, "Come on then, my boy, there's no time to waste. We'd better go and meet this Soli and Archie to see what we can do to help. I'll go on ahead as I can get to the Oosha by telekinesis. I'll wait for you there."

Vastator almost pushed him out of the bar and left him in a flash. Julian was a little bemused by his alacrity but as he set off to pick up his TAM that he had left in his flat, he thought how lucky he was to have such a good friend.

Vastator smiled grimly to himself as he positioned himself behind a pillar in the temple to wait for Archie and Soli. While he was waiting, he thought through his plan. By the time Julian had arrived, his business with the other two would be finished. He would meet Julian at the entrance to the Oosha and tell him that Soli had gone back to Altair and left a message for Julian that he was to find the drugs and take them back to Altair. Vastator would help him and insist that he go back to Altair with Julian so that he would appear to be the hero as he had originally planned. Vastator relaxed and reflected that his quick thinking might have just have got him out of trouble.

Chapter Eighteen

Mr. M

Like Vastator, Mr. M had been enjoying a drink in the early evening on the deck of his yacht in the Brighton Marina. But the difference was, he was sipping champagne from a crystal glass in privacy and unlike Vastator, his peace of mind was not going to be disturbed. Everyone called him Mr. M after his palatial boat "The Minerva," but few people knew his real name. He had just arrived one day in his boat and soon established connections with the criminal underworld. He turned his face towards the sun, enjoying the warmth on his face and stretched like a cat. He was extremely pleased with the way in which everything had panned out.

Paul studied Mr. M surreptitiously while he savoured the excellent vintage champagne. Mr. M was a handsome man, with a fine physique and tall with the chiselled good looks of a film star. His hair gleamed golden in the evening light and the sun reflected in his blue eyes made the colour more intense. He somehow had a presence that was powerful and awe inspiring and Paul had never felt able to question his origins or real name. Mr. M's high cheekbones hinted at his Russian origin and he suspected that he was one of the new rich Russian oligarchs, probably with Mafia connections, but beyond this he had no other information about his boss. He wondered if this was why he was planning to take the Faberge eggs. Perhaps his buyer had contacted him through his Russian associates. However, he didn't probe any further because from his own past military background, Paul believed strictly in the 'need to know' principle and too much information could be a very dangerous thing. It was much safer not to know some things.

"We've had the awning put around the manhole in the Steine and so far no-one has questioned it being there."

"Excellent. What about the fire alarms at the bank?"

"That has gone exactly to plan. The alarms have gone off every day but no fault has been found and so the Bank Manager has reported this to the Alarm Company and they are coming after the weekend to inspect the system and may replace it."

Mr. M nodded and smiled at Paul. "Everything okay with the tunneller?"

"Yes. I spoke to him today and the tunnel is now in place so all he has to do is set the explosive to blow a hole into the bank vault."

"Good, good. Has the other man who was helping him been paid?"

"Yes, that's all been taken care of."

"And you are sure that we can trust him?"

"He does not know anything apart from the fact that he has helped to dig a tunnel. He does not know why, or either of our names. He has a family and I made it clear that they would be under threat if he breathes a single word about the job."

"Fine."

"So, you have arranged to meet John Hallorhan at the Cinema and when you have the eggs, you'll come to the boat immediately. The crew has made all the arrangements with the Harbour Master and we sail on the tide at 7:00 pm."

The two men relaxed as the boat rocked gently in its moorings, soothed by the motion and the soft lapping of the water. The Minerva was the largest boat in the Marina and had evoked a great deal of interest from the other boat owners. Paul could see people on the balcony of the Seattle Hotel pointing to them and staring. Mr. M did not seem to notice and Paul thought that maybe he was so used to curious stares that he had become immune.

"Okay, Paul, everything seems to be in order, so I'll see you tomorrow sometime before seven. Don't be late or you'll miss the boat." Mr. M chuckled. "We're heading for the Med and you will be our guest until we reach Marseilles, where we'll stop to let you disembark."

"Thank you. That will be perfect as I can visit my sister who has a villa on the Costa Brava. I'll hire a car and it won't take me long to drive to her."

"It's my pleasure. It'll be good to have you aboard."

Paul knew when he was being dismissed and climbed down the ladder and jumped on to the quayside. He had hoped that Mr. M would invite him to join him for dinner as he had an excellent chef on board, but he thought it of no matter since he would have a chance to sample the cuisine over the next couple of days. He whistled softly to himself as he sauntered back to his car in the car park.

Chapter Nineteen

The Trap

Ally leaned perilously out of Zonah's bedroom window peering up the road looking for Archie.

"No I can't see him. It's half past eight. He should be back by now."

She anxiously checked her mobile phone for the tenth time to make sure it was switched on.

"I can't understand what's taking him so long. He only had to give Signet the message. It can't have taken this long. Something must have happened to him. What are we going to do if he just disappears? We've kind of tricked both our parents into thinking that he is at the other one's house. We're going to be in big trouble."

Zonah tried to reassure her friend, emphasising every word. "Look, nothing's happened to him. He'll ring you in a minute. He's with Signet so he'll be quite safe."

Ally looked at her friend. "I just have this feeling that he's in terrible danger."

Zonah put her arm round Ally. "He'll be alright. You'll see. He's with Signet and he'll protect him."

Ally's feelings had been right. Archie *was* in danger and what's more, he did not have Signet with him. As Soli and Archie rematerialised in the Oosha, Archie shook his head to clear it.

"You okay, my boy? We'll just take a breather for a few minutes and then get on our way. You can go home to bed. You look as if you need a good sleep. This space travel wears you out, but you'll be as right as rain in the morning. I'll head for the pharmacy at the hospital and then go straight back to Altair."

Archie opened his mouth to say that the pharmacy would be closed at this time, when a voice boomed out. "Good evening, gentlemen. I'm afraid that's not quite what is going to happen. I'm sorry to say I shall have to change your plans."

Both Soli and Archie jumped in fright at the unexpected voice.

"Who's that? Come out and show yourself." Soli commanded.

Vastator appeared from behind the pillar, camouflaging his pent up energy by lounging against it casually as if he was just having an everyday conversation.

"It's Vastator," Archie told Soli.

"Well, you're a rum sort of fellow lurking in the shadows and frightening folk out of their wits. Have you come to help us?"

Vastator laughed. "No, I've come to stop you." Without pausing, he pointed his finger at Soli and said a few words. Soli crumpled into a heap on the floor.

Archie gasped in horror. "What have you done to him, you evil maggot? You've killed him."

"No, I haven't killed him. He'll just sleep for twenty-four hours, which will give me time to put my plans into action. But I could murder you, you interfering boy, you always turn up at the wrong time, always prying and meddling in things that don't concern you. Yes, perhaps I *should* just get rid of you."

Archie had rearranged Soli's prostrate body on his side in the recovery position that he had learnt when he earned his First Aid badge in the Cubs. Vastator stepped up to Archie as he spoke, and lifted him up by his shirt collar his face close to Archie's.

"Get away from me, you slimy snotball, you piece of primeval sludge, you dog turd."

Vastator let out a long chuckle that seemed to echo eerily right round the temple and then he dropped him on the ground. "You're lucky, I've decided that if you went missing, it would cause too much of a hullabaloo. There would be police and helicopters all over and that's just what I don't want. No, I shall escort you to your house and I'll cast a spell. I'll put an invisible shield around the house preventing you or Ally from leaving. Your mother and father have gone away for the night and the spell will only be broken when an adult enters the house. When your parents return tomorrow night, you will be free to go out. By then it will all be too late and I will have my own Theolite, my own Philosopher's Stone, and my own Grail."

Archie was relieved that Vastator was not going to murder him but was amazed that Vastator thought that Theolite was the Philosopher's Stone, and what was all that about the Grail?

"Theolite isn't the Philosophers Stone; it doesn't turn base metals into gold." Archie had been about to tell Vastator the true properties of the stone, but he stopped himself just in time. He didn't want to give away any information to Vastator that he could use.

"Yes, yes and I suppose that your name isn't Archie either. Enough. I'll escort you to your back door. I know you have a key, so you can let yourself in and just count yourself lucky that I'm in a good mood. I'll be watching you, so don't try to run away or I'll cast another spell and make you into a deaf and dumb mute."

When Archie crept into the house, he found it all in darkness and strangely quiet, so he realised that it was true: his parents must have gone away for the night. He put on the hall light and went upstairs to his bedroom. He felt numb. Vastator had outwitted them. He stared glumly at the window and thought he would try to climb out, just in case the spell was a lie and a ploy to keep him a prisoner. He opened the window and put his hand out. He met a resistance like an invisible wall. Archie groaned. The spell was real and he was a captive in his own house. For the first time since he had returned, he remembered Ally and Zonah and took his mobile phone out of his pocket. Vastator must have thought that Ally was at home, and if Archie could reach her on his mobile, there might be a way of saving the whole situation.

He wondered if he would be able to use the phone and dialled

Ally's number with trepidation. To his surprise the phone gave two rings and Ally answered at once.

"Hello. It's me. I've just come back from Altair."

"Oh, Archie, thank goodness! I was so worried. I thought something had happened to you. Where are you? I thought you were coming over to Zonah's."

Archie quickly told her all that had happened.

Ally was gasping and shouting as he told her the whole story, and he could hear Zonah in the background saying, "What's happened? What's the matter?"

"By the way Ally, where are Mum and Dad? The house was all dark when I came in, and Vastator told me they had gone away for the night."

"Oh, yes. When I asked Mum if we could have a sleepover, she said that she and Dad would nip up to London and stay with Auntie Lynne."

Archie was disappointed. He thought that if his parents had gone out for the evening, they would come in later and that way the spell would be broken.

Oh well, Ally, this is what we will have to do. You two go to Hollingdean woods before you go to the Brighton Festival Parade. Find Rufus and send him over to rescue me. I'll go back to the Temple and find Soli's communicator to get the name of the antibiotics. Then I'll go to the hospital pharmacy and use the piece of Theolite I've got to make myself invisible. I know how to use the TAM to get back to Altair and I'll take the antibiotics to Signet. Now, you two will have to go to the Marina and pick up the carrier bag containing the stolen Faberge eggs and hand them into the Security Man. Are you okay with that?"

"Of course, it won't be difficult. We can do that. No trouble. But you be careful. Don't go bumping into Vastator again. He's real mean and you never know what he might do. I'll call you in the morning."

"Sleep tight and mind the bugs don't bite," Ally giggled and rang off.

Vastator had watched Archie go into the house and when he had cast the spell and was satisfied that Archie was a prisoner, he settled down to wait for Julian at the entrance to the Oosha. About half an hour later, Julian materialised in front of Vastator, who put his hand out to him, and slapped him on the back.

"Welcome, friend."

Julian asked, "Where's Soli?"

"I don't know I've been waiting here but no-one's shown up. I guess it's all down to you and me now. I know the name of the drugs that we need. We'll get them tomorrow and take them back to Altair."

Julian nodded. "Then I can introduce you to everyone and they'll give you a hero's welcome."

Vastator smiled. His plan was not ruined and everything was going to turn out just as he had schemed. Soon he would get his Grail and adulation as well!

Archie went over to his bedroom window and looked out. He could hear no sound. He could see that there was no wind as the trees were not moving, but it seemed eerie, as he could usually hear distant sounds at night: a train, a police siren, an urban fox bark, a car revving it's engine up, muttering dislocated sentences from passers-by reaching a crescendo and receding as they walked away. He supposed that the barrier had blocked out these sounds. It gave him the creeps as he imagined it was like a large transparent bubble around the house that could implode at any moment, reducing the house and everything in it to a pile of dust.

Archie felt very alone. He looked up at the sky and drew comfort that Altair was out there somewhere. The sky was a midnight blue festooned with sparkling stars like lights on a Christmas tree. As he scanned the sky, a shooting star streaked across it, from right to left, like a zipper opening up and revealing the naked universe and then closing again. Archie's spirits soared. It was supposed to be lucky to see a shooting star. He took it as a good omen for the next day. He jumped into bed; his optimism restored and immediately fell into a deep sleep.

Chapter Twenty

The Prisoner

Archie woke up early. It was barely light. He felt disorientated and, for a moment, could not remember where he was. He had been dreaming of Altair and he thought he was still there. He jumped out of bed feeling full of energy. He had things to do. He remembered his grandfather's favourite saying, well it was more like a rule really and it had become a family motto. *Hope for the best but plan for the worst.*

He had no reason to doubt that the girls would find Rufus who would be able to set him free so he could speed to the hospital pharmacy in a couple of hours. He knew he could just sit tight and wait, but he wasn't doing that. He was hoping for the best but planning for the worst.

He had a quick shower, dressed and emptied out his rucksack so he could load it with the antibiotics. He went downstairs and helped himself to a large bowl of cornflakes. He tried the back door just in case Vastator had missed it, but it was no good. The door opened but when he tried to go through the doorway, he met an invisible force. Once he had finished his breakfast, he started to look around for a tool of some sort to see if it would pierce the unseen screen. He found a screwdriver in the kitchen drawer and opened the back door and tried it, but it was no good. It just seemed to push it a little way and then stop. Scissors didn't work either.

He went upstairs and opened his bedroom window. He had an idea. He would try and attract Jazz's attention. Jazz, whose real name was Charles Razzle, was formerly a Spitfire pilot and had helped Archie before. They had become good friends and Archie often went over to see him. They both liked archery and Jazz had set up a target in the garden where they spent many happy hours. Jazz had built himself a small house in his large garden and had given the house to his son and his family. Archie could just see the small house from his bedroom and he tried shouting Jazz's name. After about five minutes, he realised that it was no good. He was too far away for Jazz to hear him. He didn't know Jazz's phone number and he remembered that he had told him that his number was ex-directory so he couldn't contact him by phone.

Across the City, Ally had also woken up early and was washed and dressed before her friend Zonah had even got out of bed. She told a sleepy Zonah that she was just going to nip down to the woods to try and find Rufus. Zonah nodded and said she would tell her Mum that she had just gone to the local newsagent to buy some crisps and Coke to take with them to the park. Ally crept down the stairs and slipped out of the front door, closing it carefully behind her so that it did not slam. She ran up the road, and crossed the street, and ran past the swing park into the woods.

The sun was shining. It had rained in the night and Ally took deep breaths of the fresh-smelling air. She had brought her mobile with her and rang her brother. The message came up "No signal" and Ally thought it must be the woods. She would call Archie when she went back to Zonah's house. She walked the last few steps to the tree with five branches and looked around. A gentle breeze carried the sound of birds singing. A few drops of rain occasionally plopped on to the ground, shaken nonchalantly from boughs of cupped leaves. Apart from that it was quiet and still.

Ally shouted in her mind, *"Rufus, Rufus."* She felt her call break the serenity of the woods." *Rufus, Rufus!"* she repeated her shout a little louder. She was just about to shout again when there was a flurry of wings flapping and Nessie landed on one of the branches of the tree and said crossly.

"Good heavens, you silly girl, whatever are you doing making such a terrible noise at this time of the morning? Don't you know that the chicks and youngsters are still sleeping? I expect you've woken them all up."

Ally felt the parakeet's anger in her mind like a slap. *"Oh I'm so s — s — sorry but it's just that Archie is in trouble and we need Rufus to help him."* She was quite taken aback at Nessie's reprimand, but in the next moment she felt the bird's consciousness wash over her gently.

"Sorry, my child, I shouldn't have shouted at you. Carry on."

Ally was reassured and quickly went on to explain what had happened while all the time Nessie was scrutinising her with her beady eyes.

"Hmm, I see that the situation is quite urgent. Rufus never appears before midday, so I suppose I'll have to fly to the rescue. Where do you live? You'll have to give me directions from the air."

Ally thought carefully and said, *"You know Hove Park?"*

Nessie nodded her head.

"Well our road is two back from the park on the east side. Our house is quite easy to spot as it's the only one in the road with a green roof and dormer windows." Ally realised that Nessie might not see in colours, and put her hands up to her mouth. *"Oh, do you recognise colours?"*

Nessie ruffled her feathers. *"I'm not colour blind you know, and of course I can see colours."*

Ally gave sigh of relief. *"Tell Archie not to worry about the bank robbery. He'll know what you mean. Zonah and I will go to the Marina and hand the carrier bag to one of the security guards. I can't seem to get through to him on the mobile phone."*

"Okay, I'll be off then. Don't worry. I'll have him free in next to no time."

Ally watched through the gap in the trees as the parakeet rose in the air, dipped one wing like an aeroplane, turned and headed west towards Hove.

Archie had been trying to pierce the invisible shield with one of his archery arrows. It had not worked and he thought that if he used his bow to shoot the arrow, the speed might just force it through. He wrote a note to Jazz and wound it round the arrow and secured it with an elastic band. The trouble was that he would have to stand back from the window to give the arrow a chance, and he would not be able to see Jazz's door. He looked around and pulled his chest of drawers across the room into the corner opposite the window. He stood on the chest and he found that he could just see the top of Jazz's door.

As he stood on the chest, he felt Nessie approaching before he saw her. She smashed into his consciousness like a plane making a crash landing and he felt her connect with his mind.

"Whoa!"

"Sorry I didn't mean to shock you, but Ally told me that you needed help urgently."

Archie couldn't help thinking, *"Oh no, it's you. I suppose you've come to gloat."*

"I don't do gloating" She ruffled her feathers in annoyance. *"I've come to help you, and give you a message, not to say I told you so."*

Archie was relieved and looked at Nessie hopefully. The parakeet repeated Ally's message and said that she could not get through to him on her mobile phone. Archie nodded; that explained things because he couldn't contact Ally on her phone either.

"I can see you've got your bow and arrow. What were you planning to do?"

Archie explained that if he could hit Jazz's door with the arrow he had written a note to say the lock on his bedroom had broken and to ask Jazz to come in and open it from the outside because he was stuck. He had given directions to where the key to the back door was hidden. He explained to Nessie that once an adult had entered the house, the invisible shield rendering him a prisoner would disappear and he would be free. Nessie nodded while he explained.

"Ah, that's quite easy then, it must be a one-way force field designed to keep you in but others can enter, which means that I can peck a small hole in the screen from outside. It will repair itself within a minute so I cannot make a large enough hole for you to escape, but there will be just be enough time for you to shoot the arrow. Get your bow and arrow ready and when I say go, just shoot. There's a mark on the screen where a seagull has left its droppings so I'll make the hole just above it."

"Great, I've got my bow, so I'm ready when you are."

"Okay, now it will take a few minutes of constant pecking. Do try not to shoot me, won't you."

Archie never failed to rise to Nessie's bait and said, *"I'm the best archer in my club and I've won lots of contests, so I think I can shoot pretty straight."*

Nessie let out a great cackle. *"I'm mighty glad about that."* When she had stopped laughing she said, *"Now, are you ready? Alright, I'm going to start pecking now."*

Archie was poised to shoot and the thirty seconds it took Nessie to penetrate the barrier seemed like forever to him.

At last Nessie stopped pecking and said, *"Now, shoot. Now! Go, go, go!"*

Archie's arrow flew straight and true and lodged in Jazz's door with a twang. A few moments later Jazz came out, looked at the arrow and scratched his head. Then he looked up at Archie's window and Archie mimed to him that there was a message attached to the arrow. Jazz pulled the arrow out of the door, pulled the elastic band till it snapped and read Archie's note. He looked up at Archie and with a broad grin on his face and gave him the thumbs up sign.

Nessie laughed and said, "*I'll go now. You're out of trouble and my chicks will be cheeping for their breakfast. Bye for now.*"

She soared high up into the air and for a few glorious moments Archie experienced flying. He could see the houses below him growing smaller; felt the wind in his hair and the upsurge of a thermal carrying them higher. Then the link was broken and he watched Nessie growing smaller. He smiled. Maybe she wasn't such a bad old bird after all.

Chapter Twenty-One

Game On

A rchie quickly took out his Swiss Army penknife and used the screwdriver to remove his bedroom door handle. He heard Jazz calling his name as he hid the handle and screws carefully in his drawer so that he could replace them later.

"I'm up here in the back bedroom down the corridor."

Jazz followed the sound of Archie's voice and opened the door.

"Thanks, Jazz, I thought I was going to be stuck in here all day. The handle has come off and I can't find it as my room's a bit untidy." Archie smiled ruefully as he gestured with his hand to the mess of piled up jeans, T shirts, socks, books, toys, computer games, glue, sweets, chewing gum, empty crisp packets and coke tins strewn on his chair, bed and on the floor.

"Yes, it is a bit untidy," Jazz remarked as he lifted one eyebrow to emphasize his understatement.

"Mmm, I'll sort the mess out later, but I'm going to the Brighton Festival in Preston Park to meet Ally and some other friends, so I haven't got time at the moment."

Jazz looked at Archie quizzically and said, "You remind me so much of a boy I met during the war. His name was Archie too."

Archie avoided meeting Jazz's eyes and quickly said, "Oh, well, it couldn't have been me. I'm too young."

Jazz shook his head as if to clear his thoughts and Archie

98

thought that one day maybe he and Ally should tell him that they *were* the children he had been so kind to all those years ago. But now was definitely not the right time as he had an urgent mission to find the antibiotics and return to Altair before Vastator.

He jumped down the stairs two at a time and Jazz followed him. "Do you want a lift to Preston Park?" Jazz asked.

Archie knew his destination was not the park and the TAM would take him where he wanted to go faster than any car. He hesitated for a moment as it would have been great to take Jazz into his confidence and to make him an ally, but he remembered the trust that the Altairians had placed in him and decided he would be breaking a confidence if he disclosed their existence to Jazz.

"Thanks for the offer but I'm going to my friend Theo's house and his Mum is taking us to the park.

"Okay, I'll send you the bill for repairing my door and for the rescue." Jazz's eyes twinkled and Archie knew that he was only teasing him.

Archie waited until he had turned the corner of his road in case Jazz was watching him. He stopped and took out his mobile phone from his rucksack that he had snatched up during his hurried departure from the house. To start with, he needed the names of the antibiotics. He knew he could go back to the Oosha to take Soli's diary where he had noted the name of the antibiotics he needed, but he was too scared to go back there in case Vastator was lurking around. He told himself not to be so silly. After all, it was still only nine in the morning and Vastator would not have got the antibiotics yet. He was about to double back to his house when he suddenly had a brainwave. Zonah's mother was a pharmacist and she would know the names of the antibiotics they would need to cure the Plague. She would probably be able to tell him if all hospitals kept a supply of these or who else might keep them. It was worth a try.

He rang Zonah's number. A voice answered, which Archie recognised as the voice of Zonah's younger brother.

"Hello Chey, Archie here. Is your Mum there? I need to ask her something."

Archie held his breath and let it out with a sigh when Chey said, "Yes she is. I'll just get her for you." Archie heard him shout, "Mummm, Mum! It's Archie and he wants to speak to you."

"Hello, Archie, Trake here. The girls have already left. I offered to take them to the park but they said they would walk."

"No, it wasn't about that; I've arranged to meet them later. I'm doing a project at school about the Plague, you know The Black Death, and I wondered if you knew the names of the antibiotics that cured it now?"

"Yes, I can tell you that. I think its Tetracycline, but hold on a sec and I'll just check in my Mims." Archie could hear her footsteps as she walked into another room and the noise of rustling paper as she turned the pages in the pharmaceutical reference book. "Hi, are you still there? The names of the drugs that they use to treat it nowadays are Streptomycin Sulphate, Tetracycline, Chloramphenicol and Co-trimoxazole. I'll send you a text so you can get the spellings right, Okay?"

"Thanks, that's brilliant. Oh, one other thing: do they have these antibiotics at all pharmacies?"

"Yes, I know that the chemist where I work has a small supply of these, but if ever there were an epidemic, the hospital pharmacies would have ample supplies. Why don't you surf the net? You'll get all sorts of information for your project."

"That's a great idea. Thanks for your help, Trake, and I'll see you later."

Trake smiled as she put the phone down. It was good to see Archie keen on doing schoolwork for a change. His mother would be pleased; she was always moaning that he left his schoolwork 'till the last minute and she had to nag him to finish projects and do homework.

Archie nipped into the driveway of a house and tiptoed down the side where he could not be seen. He took out the TAM and set it for Terra. It asked him to enter the country and so he pressed the button for United Kingdom. The TAM then gave him the options of Longitude and Latitude or Postcode. He felt pretty sure that Vastator would go to the local hospital and he did not want to risk bumping into him, so it would be safer to go to a London hospital. The only name of a hospital that came to mind was St Thomas's, as his Granddad had had an operation there. He dialled Directory Enquiries and wrote down the hospital's number. He called up the number and Archie got a reply after two rings. He groaned when he realised that it was a plastic voice saying, "All our operators are busy answering other calls but we value your call and you have been placed in a queue and we will answer your call as soon as an operator becomes free. We are sorry for the delay."

He was jumping up and down with impatience, each time that the plastic voice repeated the message. "Come on, come on answer." He was so surprised when they eventually answered that he nearly dropped the phone.

"St Thomas's, how may I help you?"

"Oh, hello, yes, I wonder if you can give me the address of the hospital and the postcode. I want to send someone a get well card."

The operator confirmed the address and postcode and continued, "Do you know the ward?"

"Yes thank you very much."

Archie picked up his rucksack and quickly entered the postcode into the TAM and pressed go.

He closed his eyes and once again experienced the strange dizzy kaleidoscope feeling that this kind of travel gave him. When he opened his eyes, he was standing on the pavement in a busy London Street, at the bottom of some steps. He looked around and saw that no one had seemed to notice his sudden appearance. There was a large sign saying St Thomas's Hospital to the right of the steps and Archie grinned with satisfaction. Now all he had to do was find the pharmacy and the antibiotics.

"Archie, Archie?" He heard a voice in his head but thought he must be imagining it." *Archie, Can you hear me?"* He looked around but could not see anyone. *"Archie, Archie."* The voice was louder and more urgent.

"Rufus?"

"Ah you can hear me."

"Where are you? I can't see you?"

"I'm far away but gifted ones can hear me from a distance."

"Cool"

"Nessie told me about your predicament and that she managed to help you escape from Vastator's web. Are you okay? Do you need any more help?"

"No, I'm fine, thanks. I'm just getting the antibiotics and I'm going straight back to Altair. Signet gave me a TAM on Altair and showed me how to use it. But I am worried about my sister and Zonah. They're going to the Marina to wait for the bank robber to make the drop and then give the Faberge eggs to one of the Security men. These men are treacherous and I think the girls may be in danger."

"I'll speak to Ally, and I arrange to be close by to protect the girls She'll be easier to contact than you. She's a natural and she has a very strong gift."

"That's good; she wants to be a Vet, so it'll help her. I'll leave it to you to protect the girls then."

Archie felt the link break and he could no longer hear Rufus. He was so worried that he could not go with the girls, but it was impossible to be in two places at once and he felt a little reassured now that he knew Rufus was going to watch over them. One of Archie's worries was unfounded. There was no chance that he would meet Vastator.

The night before, as soon as Vastator gave Julian the message, he sent a text to his uncle on Altair. He said, "Received your message and with the help of Vastator, a good friend, will get the antibiotics tonight. I am bringing him back with me and we will be in Altair within four Terra hours."

It was lucky that Thorin was in the room that had been designated for families of the plague victims when his communicator buzzed. He had been sitting with his son in the hospital ward and had to switch it off in case it interfered with the hospital equipment. He had switched it on to see if there was any good news from anyone about the plague. Instead he read Julekar's message with growing horror. He realised that something had happened to Soli and Archie and when he read Vastator's name, he banged his hand on his head and gasped, "Oh no!"

The full implication hit him. Thorin took a few deep breaths and regained his composure. His thoughts reeled as he went to find his wife Zelana and told her he was going to the Council Offices; to the Special Task Force Centre. She opened her mouth to say something and but Thorin spoke quickly "Don't worry Zelana the information that I have is so important that I have to let the others know. This could be the breakthrough we need and if I'm right it won't matter about the quarantine."

He used his TAM and was in the room in the Council building in a fraction of a second. He looked around and saw that everybody was using his or her communicators. There was a hum of voices but the atmosphere was calm. He spotted Signet across the room and made his way over to him quickly.

"I've just received a message from my nephew, Julekar, also known as Julian who is on Serai on Terra. He says that he received my message and he'll bring back the antibiotics in a few hours. But he said he was bringing a friend called Vastator who has been helping him."

Signet drew in his breath sharply. "I bet he has!"

"Wasn't that the name of the Immortal that Archie saw collecting rats from the sewer?"

Thorin said, half hoping that Signet would tell him he was wrong.

"Yes, that's right and he's the one who has somehow started

this epidemic. I don't know what his game is and why he wants to get to Altair, but we must stop him at all costs."

"So Julian is the one who has been helping him?"

"Well we don't know that for certain, but it certainly looks that way. He may be innocent and has been tricked by Vastator, but we can't rule out the possibility that Vastator has recruited him, bribed him and turned him to against us. We don't know. So what I want you to do is to send a reply back to Julian and just tell him to stay on Terra. Say that you are sending an important representative from Altair to meet them who will escort Vastator back to Altair. Say something like... Vastator is going to be a very important man to Altair and we want to show our respect. Tell Julian that this envoy will arrive in the Temple at three pm tomorrow. I will go back to Terra." Signet looked at his watch set at Earth time. "It's four am on Terra and that will give me time to make some preparations. I've met Vastator before and we have done battle many times. I will deal with him."

When Julian received the text back from his uncle Thorin, he was in the pharmacy of the Royal Sussex, the local hospital, collecting the various brands of antibiotics they needed. Vastator was waiting outside. Before going to the hospital, they had crept into the library at Sussex University in the dark and used one of the computers in there to surf the net and find the names of the drugs they needed. Julian found the last antibiotic on his list and transported himself to where Vastator was waiting. It was the early hours of the morning and still dark. There was no one around.

"Everything went okay?" Vastator asked him.

"Yes, I've got the drugs we need. I sent a message to my uncle and he has arranged for an important person to come in from Altair to escort you back. They want to arrange a big welcome for you because you've been so cooperative in dealing with our problem. They want us to meet them tomorrow . . . oh no, I mean today at three pm in the Temple."

Vastator had to hide his disappointment. He was anxious to

get to Altair and this delay was extremely annoying. The irritation he felt disappeared quickly as he realised he would be introduced to all the high officials of Altair *not* by a mere student but instead by a respected Spokesperson. This would suit his plans better and he gave Julian a broad grin.

"Fine, I shall have a little snooze and I'll meet you at the Temple at three."

Chapter Twenty-Two

The Bank Heist

Ally was not the only person who was out early that morning. At 7.30 John Hallohan was striding across the Old Steine heading for the striped canvas awning that had been placed around the manhole. He was not a big man, about five-ten, and lean. His friends described him as wiry and he worked out at a gym twice a week to keep himself that way. He was handsome in a rugged way with piercing blue eyes. These eyes made a quick sweep of the area. There were not many people around and those that were, were paying no attention to him in his overalls. He moved quietly inside the tent and lifted up the manhole cover. He climbed down the iron ladder effortlessly, even carrying his heavy tool kit.

Once he reached the bottom, he stood silently and alert listening for any sounds. Satisfied that there was no one in the sewers, he marched towards the side corridor. He was not afraid of the assignment and in fact he was looking forward to it. He had been a tunnel rat in Vietnam and had experience of tunnels. He guessed this was the reason that Mr. M had approached him. The Vietnamese had tunnels under their villages. Some were a century old. The tunnels went from home to home, village to village, jungle to jungle. It was the job of the tunnel soldiers to go down into them. There was a whole *other* war under the ground.

In an instant his memory carried him back forty odd years. He was in a smoky dark tunnel and his batteries were dying. He needed to move quickly to reach the end of the tunnel before the searchlight gave out and left him in the blackness. He crawled along ignoring the pain from his bloody and scraped knees, one hand holding the dim torch up and the other touching the ground to keep his balance. He could feel the terror rising. He did not look back, for he knew the enemy was behind him somewhere in the nightmare blackness. Unseen but there. And creeping up on him.

John shook his head to clear the memory. Compared to his past experiences this would be a doddle. It was too well organised for anything to go wrong. The people that had organised the bank heist had planned everything down to the last detail. His contact Paul had introduced him to his fellow tunneller, recruited just to help dig the tunnel. He called himself Pete, but John suspected that this was a protection alias. They had dug the tunnel in the previous four weeks. Every night when there was no one in the sewers they crept in. They had dug about three feet of tunnel every night. They had buckets and had brought a folding wheelbarrow with them. When the barrow was full, they took it to the main sewer and dumped the earth. It had all been worked out that the sewer could disperse this volume of earth each night. It had taken them thirty days to dig thirty yards of tunnel.

When they had finished the tunnel, they dug upwards and were delighted when they reached the underside of the vault slab made of concrete and steel. They knew that the tunnel had been the right length and that their calculations had been proved right. They had cut a circle twenty-four inches wide for the entrance to the tunnel and brought a piece of plywood pre-cut to those dimensions. Every night when they left, they packed the buckets, spades and wheelbarrow into the tunnel and put the door they had made in the hole. They caulked the edges with concrete to make it look like a capped off pipeline.

John found the circle on the wall and could see the lines of concrete where the board had been placed to conceal the opening. He opened his tool bag and took out a pair of gloves, and when he had put them on he grabbed a chisel and a large screwdriver. He chipped away the concrete, prised open the board and lifted it to one side. He took out his searchlight and snapped it on. The high power beam lit up the readymade tunnel, and he scanned the sides to make sure the way was clear and the walls had not collapsed. He grinned in satisfaction. The tunnel was still perfect and he felt a sense of pride.

He pushed the bag into the tunnel, climbed in after it and crouched in the entrance. From this position he leaned back and grabbed the edge of the board. He slid it across the gaping hole. It was unlikely that anyone else would be down here but it was always best to be cautious. He moved from his crouching position on to his hands and knees and made his way along the tunnel pushing his bag in front of him. The tunnel was short, only thirty yards long, but it was hot and airless—by the time he reached the dead end, he was bathed in sweat.

When he reached the end of the tunnel, he took out the water-cooled battery powered drill from his bag. He bolted it to the underside of the vault slab and began the arduous task of boring the two and a half inch hole through the five feet of concrete and steel. Water to cool it came from a tap previously set in the water main. John smiled at the thought that he was using the water from the bank.

After five hours of drilling and three changes of battery, John finally succeeded in making the two and a half inch hole. He could feel beads of sweat forming on his head and running in a constant stream towards his eyebrows. His T-shirt and overalls were soaked through with sweat. He put the drill away in his bag and sat propped up against the tunnel wall. He wiped the sweat from his forehead on his sleeve.

At about the time that Ally and Zonah reached Preston Park, John was taking a break to eat. He took a sandwich, crisps and a coke from the toolbox that he had brought earlier at a newsagent.

He felt refreshed after eating and drinking and put the empty coke can, crisp packet and sandwich wrapper in his bag. He did not want to leave any evidence behind that would link him to the crime he was about to commit.

Paul had given him an explosive device and he handled it carefully. He inserted it into the hole he had drilled and wedged a bar across the hole to keep in place. He stood back, happy with his work, and gave a contented smile. That would certainly blow a hole straight into the floor of the bank vault. After having set the timer for five minutes, he crawled out of the tunnel pushing his bag in front of him. When he reached the end of his tunnel he kicked the board away and scrambled out. Panting from the physical exertion he sat quietly enjoying the stillness. He checked his watch. Any minute now the device would explode.

There was a low rumble. The ground vibrated and smoke and dust belched out of the tunnel entrance. Then there was complete silence. John wasn't too worried because when the robbery had been planned, his contact had told him that they had an insider in the Bank. He had been recruited to set the alarms in the bank off every day during the past week. Of course it was always a false alarm and the Bank Manager had called in the alarm company to check the system. They were puzzled because they could find no fault with the alarm. John knew that the alarm would be set off now by the vibrations from the explosion, but the Bank Manager and the Police would just think it was part of the on-going problem with the alarm system.

It was clever but not infallible. John took out a mask and carpenters apron from his bag and put them on. He made his way back up the tunnel. Inside was a dark mist and he could see particles of dust floating in the air, caught in the light from his torch. He fixed the beam where he had placed the explosive and it revealed a large hole. He could see right into the bank vault. It was perfect. The pile of rubble from the foundations of the vault was large and he stood on it and pulled himself up and through the space into the vault.

He found the box he wanted and quickly used a piece of wire to open the lock. A minute later the door sprung open and, just as Paul had described, there were two medium-sized boxes. He lifted them out and placed them carefully in the two pockets of the carpenter's apron. He looked around longingly at all the deposit boxes. He had been told just to open number 199 and take the Faberge eggs. It was very tempting, but he didn't want to spend any more time than he had to inside the vault. His heart was beating fast. Someone could still investigate the alarm and check the vault and he didn't rate his chances if they did. He sat on the edge of the hole with his legs dangling down, pushed off with his gloved hands and slid down the pile of rubble.

John need not have worried. Mr Morgan the bank manager was infuriated when the Police called him to say the alarm at the bank was going off again. He was in the middle of his lunch with his family and he banged the receiver down into its cradle and stomped out to his car. He was held up by the traffic build up from the Festival Parade. It was a very hot and bothered Mr Morgan who arrived at the bank after thirty frustrating minutes. He drew up on the pavement behind the police car and jumped out of his car.

He said to the two young policemen, "It's okay, Officers," as he wiped the sweat off his brow with his handkerchief. A few passers-by had stopped to stare, wondering if they were going to witness a bank robbery. "The alarms have been going off all week. There's a dammed fault in the system. I'll just turn them off and I'll have to call the alarm people out tomorrow."

The policeman said, "Right, we've checked the outside and there's no sign of a break in."

He watched while Mr Morgan opened the bank doors, went in, and switched off the alarm. "Thanks, Officers, I'm sure everything is okay. I'll have to contact the alarm people tomorrow. The sound and movement sensor must be off balance."

Calling goodbye, he got into his car and drove off thinking about his wife's Dutch apple pie, which melted in the mouth. The policeman and his companion took another call on their radio and drove off, sirens wailing and blue lights flashing. The small crowd dispersed, disappointed that the show was over.

John made his way back through the sewers to the iron staircase and came out through the manhole. He took off the apron and then his overalls. He took out a clean T-shirt and a pair of jeans from the bag and put them on. He used the leg of the overalls to rub the dirt and dust from his shoes. He stuffed the overalls in his tool bag and then carefully laid the two boxes on the top. He peered out of the awning to check that no one was around. The coast was clear and he came out and walked away, nonchalantly blending in with all the locals. No one would have guessed that he had just carried out a daring bank heist. And no one would have guessed that he was carrying a priceless pair of Faberge eggs.

Chapter Twenty-Three

The Pharmacy

Archie bounded up the steps two at a time and passed through the automatic entrance doors. There was a large notice with arrows pointing to the different departments of the hospital. An arrow pointed to the left, which said Pharmacy. He made his way in the direction the arrow pointed and stopped when he saw a small empty consulting room. He made sure there were no doctors or nurses lurking around and he slipped inside. The door closed behind him automatically, and he took out the piece of Theolite that created the force field making him invisible. Holding out his rucksack, he experimented to see when it became invisible to find the range of the force field. He did not want people to see his bag floating through the air. Establishing that the radius of the field was about two feet, he clutched his backpack to him and slipped out of the door. The corridor led to some swing doors that opened into an area that looked like a doctor's waiting room. A woman shot round in the direction of the sound and then seemed a little confused. Archie realised that she could not see him, only the door opening and closing and he almost started to giggle at the expression on her face.

People were sitting around, some in dressing gowns and some in ordinary clothes, waiting for prescriptions. At one end of the room there was a counter and there were rows of seats facing it. Archie noticed that patients were handing in sheets of paper and being given a ticket. Every now and then a white-coated pharmacist shouted out someone's name, checked their identity, and handed over packages of varying sizes.

Archie could see a glimpse of the pharmacy through the counter opening. It looked just as he expected, with rows stacked from floor to ceiling with drugs. The pharmacists were bustling up and down the rows of medicines searching out the ones they needed. Archie hoped the ones he wanted were not on the top shelves. Entering a number in the security device on the wall by the side of the door operated the entry door next to the counter. Archie did not have to wait long before a woman in a white coat came through the doors of the pharmacy and headed for the inner door. He positioned himself behind her and slipped inside before the door closed. The door had an automatic closing device and when it clicked shut, he let out a sigh of relief, which she would have heard if she had not started up a conversation with a colleague by the counter.

Archie walked down the first row and discovered that the drugs were in alphabetical order. He followed the first rows containing A's and B's and turned the corner to the next row containing the C's. He nearly bumped into a pharmacist coming out of this row and had to jump back and flatten himself against the shelves. Archie let out a "Phew" when he had gone past and the man turned towards the sound. Archie held his breath and the man, seeing nothing, continued on his way. Two of the antibiotics began with the letter C and he took out the piece of paper to check the names. He worked his way down the aisle finding strange sounding drugs beginning with CH's and he scanned up and down until he found the shelf label reading Chloramphenicol. Luckily it was at the bottom of the shelves and he loaded fifty packs into his rucksack. He found the next antibiotic called Co-trimoxazole fairly quickly and took fifty packs of this drug. Archie consulted his list and found that the other two drugs began with the letters S and T.

Streptomycin sulphate was easy to find and he scooped up

about 50 packets and threw them into his backpack. There was sweat dripping down his forehead and he stopped to take a breather and used his sleeve to wipe it away before it dripped into his eyes. He pushed his hair back that always flopped over his forehead. It was quarter past eleven and he was pleased that he had managed to collect the drugs so quickly.

The last drug was Tetracycline and he spotted the name he was looking for at the top, just as he had been dreading. He went back to the last aisle where he had seen a footstool. He made sure there was no one around and started to push it up the aisle with his foot. It was on wheels and so it was easy. He was just about to manoeuvre it round the corner to the spot where he had found the last antibiotic when one of the pharmacists passed the end of the row and saw the footstool moving.

It appeared to be waltzing down the row on its own and she said, "Blimey, I always thought this place was haunted," and sauntered on, singing the theme song from Ghostbusters.

Archie stopped the stool and had to put his hand over his mouth to stop the giggles bubbling up from within. Changing his plans, he was going to try and climb up the shelves when he spotted a stick with grabbers on the end, just like the one that the local corner shop used to reach items on their top shelves. It was near the counter, and when no one was close, Archie picked it up and ran as fast as he could to the row where the "T's" were found. He gave a sigh of relief as he nipped into the aisle without being spotted. He reached up and grabbed a pack of twenty of the drugs and stuffed them into his rucksack. He balanced himself and reached for another pack when a pharmacist came round the corner. She saw the stick positioned in mid air and gave an ear-piercing scream and ran. Archie stretched up and took another pack of the drug. He could hear a commotion going on.

The pharmacist was shouting, "I tell you this place is haunted, I just saw the handle we use floating in mid-air taking some drugs down from the shelf."

Someone was trying to calm her down and making soothing

noises. "There, there, I think you must have imagined it. You've been doing too much overtime. Caroline, be a love, go and make her a cup of tea. I'll go and look. Which row did you see the grabber floating around?"

"It was the S and T row."

Archie propped the grabber up against the shelves and sped to the back of the pharmacy. He did not wait to see what happened next. The pharmacist's blood-curdling scream had unnerved him. He could feel sweat running down his legs under his jeans and he started to shiver with fear. He wanted to get away as soon as he could, before he was discovered He quickly made his way out of the hospital and shutting his eyes, he pressed the buttons on his TAM to take him back home. In an instant he was standing in the street near to his own house. It was only then, when he knew he was safe, did he see the funny side of the floating grabber stick. The relief made him relax. He stopped shivering and burst into fits of laughter.

Chapter Twenty-Four

The Marina

"*A*lly?"

Ally felt Rufus linking into her consciousness. "*Rufus? Where are you? I can't see you.*"

"*I'm not near you, but I can connect and communicate with you wherever you are.*"

"Cool."

"*That's what your brother said.*"

"Archie? Have you spoken to him? Is he alright?"

"*He's fine and on his way to Altair with the antibiotics. He asked me to wish you good luck and said that he'll come back to the Oosha with Signet. He asked you to meet him there.* "

"Good. Zonah and I will go back to the Oosha after we've been to the Marina."

"*Archie asked me to help you. He explained the plan to me. What time will you be at the Marina?*"

"Two o' clock."

"*Ok. There's a sewage pipe that goes to Peacehaven and luckily there's an inspection walkway that runs to the Marina. I'll be able to use that. There's an exit that comes out in Duke's Mound. I'll wait there and if you are in trouble just call my name.*"

"Don't worry, I'll shout so loud people at the Pier will be able to hear me."

"*No, don't shout.*" Rufus laughed. "*You'll burst my eardrums.*

The gift is very strong in you. I could hear you if you whispered."

"Wow."

"Bye for now."

As Ally felt the link with Rufus fade, she held her head up high. She felt both proud and awed at the same time. Signet had bestowed her with an ability and she was elated that Rufus considered that she had a talent for this skill they called the "gift".

Ally turned to Zonah and said, "Shall we go now? It's a bit early but I can't seem to relax and look at any more stalls. I've got butterflies in my stomach like before an exam."

"Me too. As Archie would say, let's do one."

Ally smiled at hearing her friend use one of her brother's expressions, and picking up her backpack she headed for the southernmost exit. Zonah followed her and they were soon walking down Beaconsfield Road to the bus stop. Luckily they did not have long to wait for a bus. The bus sped down the special bus lanes to the Old Steine and they jumped off the bus opposite St James Street. Ally noticed the striped awning around the manhole and gave a shudder of fear. She knew this was part of the robber's plans and now it was all up to Zonah and her to save the Faberge eggs.

When the pair of them reached the Palace Pier, they stopped to put on their roller boots. The sea sparkled in the sunlight, dappled like an impressionist painting. There were people splashing about in the water and a soft sea breeze carried the sounds of their laughter and shouts. The gentle wind also carried the music from a roundabout on the lower promenade. Seagulls spread their wings and cried out with glee as the thermals carried them effortlessly this way and that. Their distinctive cries added to the seaside symphony.

"Oh, I'd love to just go and jump in the water. I'm so hot and it looks so inviting."

The two girls slipped on their backpacks and set off along the wide promenade gliding smoothly, as if they had been born with wheels on their feet. Ally heard a sound behind her.

"Look, Zonah, it's the train from Volks railway. Let's see if we can race it."

For a few minutes the girls skated neck and neck with the train, until it picked up speed and drew away from them. The kids sitting at the back waved enthusiastically and the girls smiled and waved back. Born and bred in Brighton, they had often ridden back and forth in it along the beaches of Brighton. Nowadays they were quite blasé about the very first electric train to operate in the world. After all, they were ten years old and had outgrown such simple pleasures. Volks railway was strictly for the tots, trippers and train spotters. Or so they thought.

They reached the Marina early and whiled away the time by looking at the boats and deciding which ones they liked best, and which had the best names. When it was two o' clock they set off back to the Cinema complex, entered the large foyer and looked around to see where the security men stood. Satisfied that they could locate them easily, the pair tucked themselves behind the sweet dispenser. Armed with bags to look authentic, they pretended to choose the confectionary they wanted to take with them to enjoy while watching a film.

Ally nudged Zonah and whispered, "I think that's him, the American. I'm not sure. I only caught a glimpse of him in the sewers, but he has got a Safeway carrier bag. Hold on."

Ally moved round the dispenser so that she could get a better view of the man without arousing his suspicions.

"Yep, it's him. He's looking round the reception area at the waste disposal bins. Right. Move round, he's coming this way."

The two girls hardly dared to breathe in case he had spotted them. After about thirty seconds they peered out from their hiding place.

"Look, Zonah! He's left the carrier bag. Come on quick, we've got to pick it up and hand it to that Security Guard over there." Ally picked up the bag and skated up to the Security Man.

"We found this bag over by the dustbin," Ally said, holding out the carrier bag

"We thought we'd better hand it to you in case someone's lost it," Zonah added.

"You should have left it there, and come to fetch one of us. It could be a bomb."

Ally was about to say that it was not a bomb when a smooth voice from behind her said, "Thank you so much. It's my bag. I put it down while I went to buy a drink."

She looked at the man in horror. This wasn't supposed to happen! For a moment, time seemed to stand still like an image fixed on a screen when a video sticks. The man gripped her tightly on her shoulder and reached out to take the bag.

This jolted Ally back to reality as if the film had started rolling again at double speed and she cried, "Noooooo!"

She threw the bag to Zonah who was nearer the door. Zonah looked surprised but luckily she caught it.

"Run!" Ally shouted. Zonah need no further urging and went out the doors skating fast. The man was momentarily distracted as he watched Zonah streaking away and Ally broke away from him. She lurched forward and almost fell but regained her balance and skated furiously after her friend.

They could hear shouts behind them. "Stop! Thief! Stop those girls! They've stolen my bag."

Everyone stood and stared at the girls being chased and some put their hands out to stop them, but the girls swerved and ducked and managed to avoid capture. As they went round the corner, Ally called out to her friend, "Quick, go into the garage and we can double back past the Cinema. The old entrance to the Marina is still there, 'cos the workmen use it. We'll never make it up the exit road. It's too steep to skate up. The boots will be no use on the hill. We'll be caught easily."

"If we take our boots off and put on our anoraks, we'll look different and maybe they won't recognise us," Zonah said hopefully.

The girls skated back towards the Cinema, but this time under cover of the garage. They huddled between two the two last cars in the row that backed on to the wall and hastily changed their boots for their shoes.

They undid their ponytails and shook their hair loose. Peering out over the car roof, they were reassured that their pursuer was not in sight. They squeezed through the narrow gap between the wall and the boot of the last car.

"Phew, I thought we'd had it for sure," Zonah said.

"Well, I wasn't going to give up that easily," Ally replied.

They both took a deep breath and sauntered out of the car park exit. They both wanted to run but knew if they did they would draw attention to themselves. As they strolled past the entrances to the Cinema foyer, they saw that the hullabaloo seemed to have died down and they walked past unnoticed.

Ally felt as if something was creeping up behind her. She was scared and wanted to look back to see if the man was coming after them. Any minute she felt as if she would feel his hand on her shoulder. The girls reached the end of the Cinema complex and Ally stole a glance over her shoulder.

"Oh, no," she said. "It's the American. He's just come round the end of the car park and he's seen us. Run, Zonah, run."

"*Rufus, are you there? Can you hear me?*" Ally sent out a shout in her mind.

"*Yes, I'm here.*"

"*Thank goodness. We're in trouble. We've got the Faberge eggs and one of the robbers is chasing us.*"

"*Where are you?*"

"*We're heading for the old pedestrian entrance that the workmen use. It comes out near Volks's railway.*"

"*OK. I'll meet you there.*"

Chapter Twenty-Five:

The Chase

John Hallorhan, formerly a Captain in the U.S. Army, and Vietnam tunnel rat had been feeling pleased with himself. The job had been completed with no problems. The priceless Faberge eggs had been delivered in the carrier bag as arranged and he was sauntering down towards the car park to pick up his hire car, to drive to the airport to catch his flight to Spain. A commotion interrupted his pleasant reflections. Two young girls on roller boots streaked past him as if they were being pursued by man-eating tigers, followed closely by the man that he knew as Paul. Paul was shouting and waving his arms about wildly. John realised immediately what had happened. Those same girls had been hanging around earlier when he had done a survey of the area to make sure that it was all clear. Now one of them had the Safeway's carrier bag swinging from her arm and he gave chase.

As he and Paul rounded the first corner the girls had disappeared and they ran to the next corner and looked up the exit road. There was no sign of the girls.

"Quick, they must be hiding in the garage," Paul said. The two men began to search behind the rows of cars. John reached one of the exits and looked out. The two girls were strolling brazenly down past the Cinema towards what appeared to be a dead end. He dodged back into the garage before they had a chance to look back and see him. He pointed to his car and threw Paul the keys.

"I've just seen them. You drive my car down the road past the cinema and I'll go on foot. They don't know we've spotted them yet and we can cut them off. Switch the car mobile on to loudspeaker and I'll use my mobile to keep in touch with you."

John was furious. A cold anger spread over him. How dare someone ruin all his plans? Especially two youngsters. He supposed they thought it was a prank. A trick. He'd like to show them a trick or two. He'd bang their blasted heads together. He walked out of the garage quickly and followed the girls who were some fifty yards ahead. He took out his mobile phone, dialled the car number, and began speaking to Paul.

One of the girls looked around and from her horror-struck expression he knew that she had recognised him. The two girls started to run and John broke into a run, shouting instructions to Paul down the telephone. He was gaining on them as they went round a corner.

"Right, Paul, we've got them now. They're trapped."

When he reached the corner, the road was empty. There were no girls. Then he saw a gate which said, 'Workmen and Brighton Council workers only.' He crossed the road and tried the gate; it opened and he saw the girls running down a path, which seemed to lead to the seafront.

"Okay, Paul, the little rats have found a way out. I'll follow them and you drive round to the promenade road. We'll easily catch the little devils there. It's fairly empty this far along the seafront and it's a long way to the Pier and the crowds of holiday makers."

"Rufus, are you there? Can you hear me?"

"Yes, I'm waiting for you by the workman's entrance to the Marina."

"Thank goodness, one of the men is right behind us."

"Okay, don't worry. I'll be there to help you. Nessie's here too; she insisted on coming with me."

"Good. We need all the help we can get."

The girls pounded down the walkway towards the promenade, glancing over their shoulders, hoping that the door would fool the man. They had no such luck. He came racing through the door, and what was worse; he seemed to be catching up with them. He was just a step away from Zonah and was reaching out to grab her. Ally looked around frantically for Rufus and Nessie. Out of the corner of her eye, she saw a streak come out of the sky and hurtle towards the man.

Nessie swooped at his eyes and he put his hand up to ward off her angry pecking beak. Just at that moment, Ally saw Rufus bounding across the road and as he passed in front of the man, he did a spectacular leap sideways. The man was taken by surprise and lost his balance, tumbling on to the concrete. Ally was looking back at their pursuer, but Zonah had been keeping her eyes peeled for an escape route.

"Look, Ally! There's a train coming into the station and there's a queue waiting to get on the train."

Ally and Zonah sprinted towards the crowd and tried to mingle in.

"I don't think he will dare to approach us," Zonah said with a sigh of relief. Ally looked around apprehensively and saw the man get up. A car drew up and tooted its horn and the man opened the passenger door and jumped in smartly. The girls squeezed in front of a rather large woman, trying to hide, but they could see that the men had spotted them.

"Are you all right, ducks?" she said concernedly looking back and forward from one to the other. "You look as if Old Nick himself was chasing you."

"Well, there was this man who wanted us to go for a car ride with him and he kept following us so we ran," Ally said and crossed her fingers behind her back.

The woman's face went redder and redder till it almost matched her hair. She said angrily, "Bert, Bert did you hear that? There was some pervert trying to coax these two girls to go with him. Don't you worry, girls; you'll be as safe as houses with us.

My Bert will look after you, won't you my love. Come on the train with us, and we'll make sure you get home." She indicated towards the train. "Just squeeze in beside the twins, Ad and Art. Bert and I'll sit on this side with Roa and Mia. I'm Betty by the way."

Bert was even larger than his wife and there was a lot of heaving and squirming before they all got settled, and Roa ended up sitting on Bert's lap. The driver made sure all the passengers had boarded safely, gave everyone a cheeky grin and with a 'toot toot' the train left the station.

"*Ally, I'll follow you to the pier station. Those men haven't given up. They've got in their car and are going to be waiting for you when you get off the train. I'll slink along behind all the parked cars opposite the promenade so that I don't draw too much attention.*"

Ally felt Nessie's presence. "*Hi, you guys. I'm going to head home. There's a seagull eying me up for his next meal. There are too many seagulls around the pier and I don't want to have to fight for my life.*"

"*Ooh, I didn't realise you were putting your life at risk. That was very brave of you, Nessie. Thank you.*"

Ally heard a great cackle of laughter. "*You're welcome.*" Allie felt the link break between her and Nessie.

She spoke to Rufus. "*Be careful. Try and keep out of sight otherwise it could be dangerous for you. These men are like the Terminator. They just won't give up.*"

"He's a bit of a minger isn't he?"

Ally was a little distracted as she was thinking that when this was all over, she would go to the pet shop, find out what parakeets like to eat and buy Nessie a whole sack full as a treat. She did not know what Zonah was talking about.

"Ally?"

"Sorry, I was thinking. What did you say?"

Zonah repeated her question.

"Who? Oh not the American, he was quite handsome for an oldie, but the other one, he was a minger."

124

The twins picked up the word and started to chant and giggle. "Minger, minger."

Roa addressed the twins smugly, "I bet you don't even know the word means."

Ad replied immediately, "Yes we do. Our brother George told us. It means very ugly, just like you."

"And it means mal-od-o-rous." Art joined in, pronouncing each syllable separately

"Well that's a big word, betcha don't know what it means." Roa retorted.

"Yes I do, it means smelly." And she made an elaborate play of holding her nose and saying in a funny nasal voice, "Pooh, what a pong."

Everyone laughed at her antics and Ally took the opportunity to introduce herself and Zonah to everyone, and then she asked Betty if all the children were hers and why they all had unusual names.

"Good heavens no. Roa and Mia are my nieces. The twins arrived late in our lives; all my other kids are grown up. They were a bit of a surprise, weren't they Bert?"

Bert squeezed her hand and grinned.

"We'd been to Greece on holiday you see, so I had to give them Greek names. The boy's called Adonis and the girl's Artemis. Ad and Art for short."

She gave a great laugh. Her laugh was so infectious that soon everyone joined in.

Bert gave a great chuckle and winked at the twins. "You're lucky we didn't go to Russia. Your Mum might've called you Vladimir and Tatiana."

The journey was enjoyable with this jolly family and all too soon they arrived at the end of the line, the Pier station. Zonah wished she could stay on the train forever; she was scared of these two desperate men and of what they might do. Her imagination was running wild and she thought they might have guns and could even be reckless enough to shoot them to get the bag back in their possession. Clambering off the train the girls left the station with their adopted family in a flurry amongst a crowd of people. Bert put his arms round both Ally and Zonah. His large presence made them feel a little more secure, but they were still keeping their eyes peeled for the two men.

"Come on then, I'll walk you to your bus stop," Bert said.

"Watch out, Ally. They're here."

They had just taken a few steps when Zonah saw a car draw up and the American jumped out. Then the other man abandoned the car in the coach bay and followed him. Ally turned and saw the two men closing in on them. The driver of the car drew a gun. She gave a scream and jerked out of Bert's protective arm,

"Come on, Zonah, we'll have to make a run for it."

"Ally, I'll delay the men, but you won't make it to the Police station. Go back down the sewers, I'll be following right behind you but you'll have to carry me down the ladder. It's too far for me to jump. We'll get to the Oosha through the tunnel. Signet and Archie will be back from Altair. Signet will protect us."

Zonah needed no further urging and she raced after Ally. Glancing back at Bert she shouted, "Thank you for helping us."

Bert was standing on the pavement looking bewildered. Zonah saw Rufus spring up behind the man with the gun and bite his leg. The man put his gun away and used both hands to try to release his leg from Rufus's jaw. Rufus let go and then jumped in front of him snapping at his arm, and as the man clutched his arm, Rufus let go and wound himself round his legs. The man lost his balance and fell heavily on to the pavement. Bert seemed to be galvanised into action and he tackled the American.

The last thing Zonah saw was Bert punching the American on the nose and as he reeled back from the blow, he bumped into his friend and fell over him. Ally glanced round and saw that the crowd who had gathered to watch the spectacle were laughing and pointing at Rufus as he streaked away across the road using the pedestrian crossing.

"Okay, Ally, I'm right behind you."

Reaching the workman's awning, the girls hurtled inside and flung open the manhole. Rufus joined them seconds later, and Ally picked him up and carried him under one arm as she descended into the sewer beneath.

"Phew that was close," whispered Ally.

"Why are you whispering?" Zonah whispered back.

"'Cos there might be some workers around and we're not supposed to be here."

"Okay," Zonah said in a whisper and had a fit of the giggles. The tension had been too much for the girls and once released, the floodgates opened and they both stood there laughing till the tears rolled down their cheeks.

Every time one of them stopped the other would say, "Do you remember the man's expression when we ran?" or some other funny or scary incident and they would both start laughing again.

"Come on, you two, we must get to safety. Those two men are as cunning as foxes and they may guess where we have gone."

Ally started to giggle again because it seemed so funny that a fox should use this expression. In between gasps of laughter, she told Zonah what Rufus had said and both the girls clutched their stomachs, as they were overtaken with mirth.

Meanwhile, the two men had recovered and turned on Bert. Paul was holding him down while John kicked and punched him. They did not see Betty, Bert's fiery-haired wife who had an equally fiery temper, as she descended upon them in a fury.

She started to hit John about the head with her handbag shouting, "Get off him, you pair of dirty perverts. Take that, you cowardly scumbags. And that, two against one, is it. Well you didn't reckon on me, did ya?"

Paul immediately held his arms up to protect himself from the blows that were raining down on him thick and fast and he let go of Bert. Bert was free and he leapt up and landed John with a punch. He had been aiming at his nose again but John turned his face and he caught him on the cheekbone instead. The two crooks could see that a crowd was gathering, which was the last thing they wanted.

Paul shouted, "Come on. We have to get away from here."

They both ran, and did not stop until they reached the fountain in the centre of the Old Steine. Looking around carefully for some clue to help find the girls, Paul said despondently, "We've lost them. I don't know what Mr. M is going to make of all this."

John narrowed his eyes and said, "Hang on. There's something funny about all this. I don't think the girls just went to all this trouble for a joke. I think they knew what was in the bag. The only place we've talked about the robbery and the arrangements were in the sewer. Suppose they were down there and they overhead us. I've heard of cases where kids live in the sewers. They've disappeared. It's a long shot, but if I'm right they'll be hiding in the sewers. Come on, quick."

Down in the sewers, just as the two girls were beginning to calm down and stop giggling, Ally heard a noise. They both stood stock-still and listened until the realisation hit them like a shockwave. Someone was coming down the ladder. As they heard the twang of feet on the old Victorian iron ladder, they were horrified.

"Oh no," Zonah said, "It must be the two men. How did they know we would be here?"

"Quick! We've got to reach the door to the Temple. They'll never find us there."

Rufus pounded off with Zonah and Ally following him through the passages. They bumped into each other as Rufus stopped suddenly at the blank wall. Ally stepped up to the wall.

"I think its five bricks up and ten along." She pressed the wall and nothing happened.

"Oh, quick! They're nearly here." Zonah wailed.

Frowning with concentration Ally said, "I know it's definitely five and ten, so it must be ten bricks up and five along."

She pressed the brick and a doorway opened. In the nick of time, Rufus and the two girls dove through it and heaved it shut.

Zonah's bag had slipped off her shoulder and one of the straps was shut in the door. Zonah frantically pulled at it and it slid through the crack. Leaning on the door, they stood listening for the two men.

John's sharp eyes had just caught sight of the strap disappearing and he went over to the wall and ran his hand over it,

"Look there's a crack here. There must be a door. Look. There must be a way to open it. We must find it."

They could hear the men's voices through the wall and the two girls looked at each other in dismay. Pulling her friend behind her, Ally started to run up the slightly sloping passage lit with the familiar Lumenite lamps. Rufus had run ahead up the passage.

"Come on. We can just get to the Temple and we'll be safe. Come on, Ally. Run for your life!"

Chapter Twenty-Six

The Delivery

At about the time that the girls were travelling sedately along Brighton seafront on the Volks's railway, Archie was being instantly transported across billions of miles back to Altair. Archie opened his eyes and blinked in surprise. He wasn't surprised to find himself at the entrance to the Town Hall in Altair, but he was rather taken aback to see Pauntil, Santha, Dr Hokusain, Dr Kiddush, Lev, Beshley, Asphodel, Aloric and the four Elementals with their shiny wings all waiting to welcome him.

There were two Gillyaid standing sentry at each end of the terrace, their golden manes glinting in the sun. Archie's eyes swept over the crowd and he saw Elves, Fairies, Gnomes and Leprechauns and creatures that he did not recognise all standing on the terrace. Signet was pacing up and down muttering to himself. It seemed, to Archie, that they all stared at him for ages but it was just a heartbeat. Signet and Beshley quickly moved forward and one after another gave him a hug,

Signet said, "Well done, Archie, my boy, you did a good job."

Doctor Beshley simply said, "Thank you, Archie."

Archie slipped his backpack off his shoulders and rummaged inside and handed package after package of the antibiotics to Doctor Beshley. There were more crowds of people gathered at the bottom of the steps leading to the Town Hall. They watched as Archie handed over the packages and an excited murmur ran around the crowd. They realised that Archie's mission had been successful and there were loud cheers, whistles, and the tremendous sound of stamping of hooves and feet. It all happened too fast for Archie to be embarrassed, and he smiled and gave a little bow to the crowds.

The medical team rushed off with the drugs that would save the lives of the Altairians. Thorin shook hands with Archie and someone handed him a drink. Archie was ushered into the grand entrance hall of the Town Hall and somehow Archie found himself sat in a chair.

"Will everyone be okay now?" he asked.

Signet smiled. "Yes, thanks to you. Quite remarkable. Astounding. I knew you were special." And he started to pace up and down muttering the praises to himself. Archie grinned; this was the Signet he knew.

Levi came through the door and walked up to Archie. "How is Soli? Is he all right? Signet told me what happened. I'd like to put a spell on Vastator myself, the wretched, cursed Immortal."

Asphodel approached Archie and Lev stood back in deference to their Ruler.

"I'd like to thank you on behalf of all the citizens of Altair. The Council have decided that we will award you with citizenship of our planet and freedom of the City of Uckbata. When this is all over, Signet is going to arrange for you to come back for a ceremony and we will award you with this special honour."

Archie was so astounded that he could hardly take in the enormity of Asphodel's offer. "Cool. But it was nothing. I was pleased to help."

Asphodel continued, "Your actions have saved the lives of many Altairians. It was certainly *not*, as you say, nothing. We are extremely grateful and you will always be welcome on Altair. We will help you throughout your life, and we will consider any of your requests. Anything you want, within reason, as long as it is not detrimental to you or life on Terra, we will grant. We hope you will spend many happy hours here with us."

Archie paused while he took in what the Ruler had said and hesitantly asked, "I do have a request. Can my sister, Ally and her friend Zonah come to the ceremony too? I've told them all about Altair and they would love to visit, especially Zonah 'cos she loves Unicorns."

Asphodel smiled. "Of course. That would be very acceptable. After all, half the fun of winning awards is to share the experience with friends and relatives. You may keep the TAM, communicator and piece of Theolite as you will need these in the future."

Aloric came up to Archie and gave him a wink. "Wow, you're a hero. Don't know if I can stand next to you now. "Archie grinned at him. Aloric continued, "I've just had a brilliant idea. When you come back for the ceremony with the girls, we'll have our own celebration for all the youngsters of Altair. You can ride on our backs and along the beach and we'll have a picnic. It'll be brilliant."

Asphodel nodded her approval and Signet gave Archie one of his rare smiles.

"Come on then, my boy, we had better get back to Terra. I still have work to do to break the spell that Vastator has cast over Soli and put him right about the Theolite. That wizard is becoming a nuisance in his quest for the Philosopher's Stone that will change base metal into gold. He seems to believe that it will grant him continuous eternal life on Earth, without being banished to the dark." Archie, Signet and Lev all stood together and everyone said their goodbyes.

Aloric stood back and said, "I will follow you down to Terra, Signet, in case you need some help."

"Great," Archie said, "Ally would like to see you again and you may meet Zonah, who will think you're awesome."

Archie wondered what had happened to the girls picking up the carrier bag from the Marina. He was a little worried because the men who had carried out the robbery were serious criminals. He was glad that Rufus had offered to protect them. He hoped they were all safe. Soon, Archie did not have the time to worry with the flurry of setting TAM's with the coordinates for Terra.

132

Buttons were pressed and Archie was once more whirling through space and wormholes back to Terra and Home.

Chapter Twenty-Seven

Reunions, Rewards and Retribution

A rchie had good reason to be worried. The girls were breathless as they arrived at the temple. They could hear the two men pounding after them and realised that they must have found the way to open the secret door. Vastator was lurking behind a pillar and watched the girls with idle curiosity.

"Quick, Zonah, hide under the table. We won't have time to reach the exit into the garden; they're too close."

Zonah wordlessly followed her friend and dived under the voluminous folds of the dust cloth covering and protecting the great table. Rufus slipped in beside them and all they could see were his amber eyes glowing in the dark.

Ally's mind connected to Rufus, *"Why didn't you escape while you could?"*

"I can't open the door to the garden from inside. I would have been trapped. Besides, it's possible that you may need more help from me."

Ally accepted Rufus's explanation and hugged her knees, trying to make herself as small as possible. Zonah hardly dared to breathe.

John and Paul burst through the doors to the temple, as breathless as the girls had been. The sight of the great temple brought them up sharply and both of them stood stock still, too shocked to speak.

John was the first to make a comment, "Bloody Hell, I've

never seen anything like this. What is this place? It's amazing."
He shook his head as if he could hardly believe his eyes. "You
English you never cease to astonish me. Who would have thought
there was such a place as this, down here by the sewers?"

Paul replied, scathingly, "It's not by the sewers, you dolt head.
We've climbed miles uphill. We must be in Hove by now. Look,
there's another door which must lead to the outside." Walking
towards the door, he spoke over his shoulder, "The girls aren't
here so they must have gone that way. We must find the little
minxes and get our Faberge eggs back. That's more important
than standing around admiring this underground witch's den, or
whatever it is."

By this time, Vastator was becoming annoyed and he thought
irritably, 'How dare all these people come marching through
here?' He was on such an important mission. He was on the brink
of getting hold of his personal Grail, the Theolite from Altair, his
precious object, and these interfering humans were in his way.
But when he heard the two men mention the Faberge eggs, his
ears pricked up. Maybe, just maybe, he could use this to bargain
with Signet. That is, if turned up from Altair.

He stepped out from behind the pillar and drew himself up to
his full height. "Can I help you?" he said.

Ally put her hand on her heart and mouthed to Zonah under
the table, "It's Vastator."

"What's he doing here?" Zonah whispered back.

Ally shrugged her shoulders and clutched her knees tighter.
Zonah, who had heard all about the evil entity, chewed her lip
nervously.

John and Paul both turned to look at Vastator. He was an
awesome sight in his long black coat, but Paul was not daunted
and said, "Who the hell are you?"

"I am Vastator, but some call me the Destroyer. But I think I
have what you want."

He called out as he walked up to the table. "Come out, you
two. Come out now," he said in a commanding voice.

The two men watched in fascination as the girls scrambled out from their hiding place and Zonah clutched her backpack containing the Safeway's carrier bag tightly.

Ally felt Rufus sit up as if he was going to show himself too. She quickly communicated to him, "*No, Rufus, stay hidden. The Englishman has a gun and if he sees you, he'll shoot you for sure.*"

"Give that bag to me."

Zonah hesitated and looked at Ally who nodded vigorously.

"Now!" Vastator boomed.

Zonah handed the bag to the Vastator. Just at that moment, the air seemed to shimmer and Signet and Archie materialised in front of them. They took in the situation immediately and moved over to Ally and Zonah.

Vastator addressed Signet, "Ah, my good friend, Signet. At last, we meet again."

"Yes, I was expecting to see you. You've wreaked havoc on the planet Altair, but with the help of Archie we've been able to put it all right. What is it you want? Why do you want to go to Altair? Do you think you can escape from your curse there?"

Vastator narrowed his eyes and gave Signet and Archie an evil look. "I want some of the rock that they call Theolite, you know, the Philosophers Stone, the one that can give me eternal life and set me free. Give me some and I'll give you these worthless baubles, the Faberge eggs that the humans seem to value so highly."

Signet laughed out loud. "You fool! Theolite is not the Philosophers Stone. The Philosophers stone does not exist. Is this why you started the plague on Altair? Why, you could have wiped out all life on the planet. Here, have a piece of the rock if that is what you want." Signet brought out a piece of rock from his pocket and threw it at Vastator who caught it neatly in his left hand.

"I don't believe you, you're lying. It can't be true."

Paul and John had been mesmerised, looking from one to the other, listening to the exchanges, but suddenly Paul came to life when he saw that the precious Faberge eggs were being offered as a trade. He took a gun out of his pocket and pointed it at Vastator. "Give me the bag, it belongs to us."

Everyone turned to look at Paul. Signet started to say that it was no good shooting Vastator as he could just catch the bullets, when the air shimmered again and Aloric materialised in the temple.

Aloric saw Paul pointing the gun at Vastator. Thinking he was a friend of Signet's and he was under threat, he leapt in front of the wizard just as Paul pulled the trigger. The noise of the gun was loud and the acoustics of the great temple sent echoes around the Oosha. The children looked on in horror as Aloric fell at Vastator's feet, bleeding from his chest. After the noise of the gun exploding there was absolute silence.

Vastator groaned. "Oh no." He started to feel weak and light-headed. He realised that Aloric's act of courage and kindness, far from protecting him, had once more sent him back to the abyss. The only thing that could stop Vastator was kindness. Aloric had unknowingly vanquished Vastator but paid the ultimate price with his life.

Everyone stared at Vastator. He sank to his knees and felt life ebb away from him. As the darkness and the cold descended on him, Vastator's last conscious thought was of his beloved Grail slipping from his fingers. They all watched Vastator, as he grew fainter and fainter like a ghost, until he finally disappeared.

Ally flung herself on the ground next to Aloric and cradled his head in her arms. Aloric looked into her eyes, "Signet, Trust in him. He knows what to do." He gave a deep breath like a sigh. His eyes closed and his head slumped in Ally's arms.

Ally gave a great shout and she cried as if her heart was broken. Great sobs racked her body and she was unaware that Aloric's blood was soaking into her T-shirt. Zonah had been trying to hold back her tears, but when she saw Ally crying, great tears rolled down her face and she knelt beside Ally and pulled her up. The girls clung to each other sobbing uncontrollably.

Chapter Twenty-Eight

The Aftermath

Signet quickly took charge. He saw that Paul was about to pick up the bag containing the Faberge eggs and pointed his ring at him uttering the words, "By the power of the ring, be still and know."

A light beam flashed from the ring towards Paul and he was frozen with his arm reaching out and his mouth open in a surprised gasp.

Archie had moved over to the girls. He and helped them up and put his arms round them both. "It's all right. Don't cry."

Ally and Archie heard Rufus say, "*Don't cry. Signet will sort everything out. Trust me. You'll see. I'm going to leave you now in Signet's safe hands. Signet, Can you open the door for me? Promise you'll come to see me in the woods. Both Nessie and I would be pleased to see you.*"

Ally pulled herself together and managed to say, "*Bye Rufus, thank you for all your help. We wouldn't have escaped from those men without you, and of course, we promise to come and see you soon, just try and keep us away.*"

Signet opened the door to let Rufus out and then turned and looked at the three children. "Well, you are a sorry sight. Don't worry. All is not lost. I can send Aloric back to Altair to the time before he came down to Terra. He will be alive, but he can never come back here. It's a shame, but it's not the end of the world. He

138

can live on Altair, but it just means that he won't be able to travel to Terra.

Ally and Zonah stopped crying instantly. With dried tear tracks on their faces, they smiled and the three children threw their arms around each other and did a dance on the spot. Ally shed a few more tears, but of happiness this time, and they all spoke at once: "How can you do that?"

"Well, I send his body back to Altair and set the TAM to a time before he set off."

"Wow, you can really do that?" Archie said.

"Yes, but I need to wake Soli up first so that he can take Aloric back." Signet muttered an incantation over the sleeping Sol and he yawned and stretched.

He sat up and clutched his head. "Oh, my head. It hurts. I've got an awful headache. Where am I? What's happened?"

Signet explained how Vastator had disabled him to pursue his own evil plans and told him what had happened to Aloric. He explained that he wanted him to take Aloric back and what he was going to do. Soli nodded quietly all through Signet's explanation. Signet touched him on the head and said, "Olli grampinious salve nacres."

Soli's headache immediately disappeared and he smiled at Signet and said, "Thank you." He moved over to Aloric and put his arms tightly around his chest. Signet took a few minutes preparing the TAM and then, without another word, he pressed the button. The air shimmered for a few moments and they were both gone.

There was silence for a moment and Archie said, "What are you going to do about him and where's the other one gone?"

They all looked around but the American had gone. John Hallorhan was on his way to the train station to take him to Gatwick where he planned to catch his flight to Spain. He had quickly analysed the situation when Aloric had been shot and used the confusion to slip away unnoticed. He had already been paid half of the money for the job. He did not want anything more to do with Paul, not after he had pulled the gun out. He realised just what a dangerous bunch he had got mixed up with. He thought to himself, 'I'm outta here. I've got five hundred thousand. I got time to catch my flight to Spain.' He grinned to himself. 'Why, I'll just have to buy a smaller villa.'

Signet said, "He's gone. Let him go. He's not a bad person. We'll keep track of him and send someone down from Altair to make sure he stays on the right path. Now this one, Mmm," he mused, "Now, just what are we going to do with him?"

They all looked at Paul, who was in a state of shock and standing like a statue. The three children all looked at Signet solemnly as they wondered what he was going to do.

Signet laughed and all three of them looked at him expectantly. He turned to the frozen statue that was Paul and again pointed his ring at him, he uttered strange sounding words and he disappeared.

"There I have cast a spell over him to compel him to go to the Police and confess all that he has done, including shooting a Unicorn that appeared out of nowhere, battling with wizards and having the Faberge egg that he arranged to have stolen from the bank snatched from his grasp by two young girls on roller boots." Signet laughed even more loudly and after all the stress of the last ten minutes, the children began to giggle.

The laughter was a release and every time one of them stopped one of the others would say, "Can you just imagine the Policeman's face?" or, "What will he do when the spell wears off and he realises that he's at the Police Station?" They would all fall about, clutching their sides as the laughter rocked through them. Signet let them laugh as he knew what they had all been through and laughter was the best healer.

"Oh, I wish I could be a fly on the wall," Archie said.

Signet looked at them all quizzically. "Would you like to watch the scene at the Police Station?"

"Oh, yes!" they all cried in unison.

"Well we can view it all on the mirror on the wall there. It's more than just a mirror. I'll just have to tune it in."

Chapter Twenty-Nine

The Magic Mirro

The children crowded round Signet as he pressed a button hidden by the mirror's ornate frame. A control panel slid out from under the mirror and Signet pressed a button.

A voice spoke, "Good Afternoon, Signet Eolzig. I will switch to viewing mode."

The mirror transformed into a screen. "Please enter the address to be viewed."

The children stared in amazement and Archie said, "Wow."

Signet's voice echoed round the temple, "Police Station, John Street, Brighton."

The screen flickered and the children could see the front office of the Police Station. "Do you want multi-viewing?"

Signet replied, "Yes."

The screen flickered once again and then showed the front office in two screens. One was the view from the Police side and the other from the civilian side.

Signet addressed the children, "This is from Altair using their most up-to-date technology. We had it installed recently and all us wizards have found it very useful."

The children watched the screen with interest. There was a small man with a balding head complaining about the noise his neighbours made at one booth, but the other one was empty. They were getting quite absorbed in the man's story when Paul flung open the doors dramatically and strode up to the empty booth at the counter.

The small man glanced at him. "Get him, Drama queen." he snapped dismissively. When no one came to attend to Paul immediately, he began to tap his fingers impatiently. The other man turned to face him, glared at him, turned back to the Policewoman who was noting his complaint, and raised his eyebrows. Paul, growing even more impatient, banged on the glass. The other man, incensed by this behaviour turned to him. "Look, I've come here to report my noisy neighbours and I don't need any more noisy neighbours. Just shut up and wait your turn."

The man started to shout, "You don't understand! I want to confess to a crime. I stole the Faberge eggs from the Bank, and then two young girls wearing roller boots snatched them from me. I chased after them to the sewers, and followed them into a temple. It was terrible, there were two wizards and then a unicorn appeared out of nowhere, and I shot him. One of the wizards faded away. It was horrendous, horrendous."

That set Ally off and soon they were all clinging to each other laughing helplessly as they watched the small man's expression on the screen.

They were still giggling when a Desk Officer came to the booth. "Can you give me your name, Sir?"

"Paul Denby."

"What can I do for you, Mr Denby?

The man repeated a garbled version of his story and added, "You must arrest Mr. M. He's on his yacht called 'The Minerva' at the Marina. You must catch him. He's behind all this. He organised the robbery."

"I see, Paul. May I call you Paul?"

Paul nodded.

"So you recruited a certain Mr. John Hallorhan to tunnel into the bank vault of the Royal Bank of Scotland through the sewers. He was supposed to deliver the stolen Faberge eggs to you, at the

Marina, but two girls snatched the carrier bag containing the said eggs. You and John chased the girls who disappeared through a manhole into the sewers. And then you what?

"I've told you, already! They went through a secret door which led to an enormous temple."

"I see, and then what happened?"

The man noticed that everybody had stopped talking and were listening in on their conversation. Two Police Officers behind the counter lingered around pretending to leaf through papers so they could listen in to the interesting conversation. Paul looked around nervously and whispered his reply to the Policeman.

"So let me get this straight, Paul. There was this wizard and the two girls. Then another wizard and a boy appeared out of thin air. Is that right?"

Paul nodded in agreement.

"You had a gun and you threatened to shoot the first wizard unless he returned your carrier bag containing the Faberge eggs, which he had taken from the girls."

"Okay, Paul, and then what happened?"

Paul was getting extremely irate. "I've told you! The wizard said I couldn't kill him with a gun, but I didn't take any notice so I aimed at him but a bloody unicorn jumped out of nowhere in front of the wizard and I killed the unicorn!"

The two Policemen behind the counter, started to grin, enjoying the performance.

"So, Paul, if we investigate your story, we'll find a dead unicorn in the sewers?"

"Yes. No. I mean, the wizard sent him back to his own planet where he was going to be alive."

"I see, and where exactly is this planet, Paul?"

"I think it's called Altair and its millions and millions of light years away."

The two Policemen stopped any pretence of working and laughed out loud. The man in the next-door booth had stopped

143

talking to the Policewoman and had been following the conversation.

He turned back to her and said in a stage whisper, "He's certifiable."

The children watching the scene were falling about in helpless giggles.

The Policeman was trying to stop his mouth from turning up."I see, Paul, that's quite a story. Why don't you just go home and sleep it off. It is an offence to waste Police time you know, and I could take you into custody, but I'm prepared to let it go for now. If you still feel the same in the morning, come back by all means."

The children groaned and started to shout at the screen. "Nooo! Don't let him go. Put him in the cells. Find out if the bank has been robbed."

At that moment, two things happened almost simultaneously. The other Desk Officer whispered something to her colleague and they stepped back from the booths. "I think there was a report of the bank alarms going off this afternoon, but they had been having trouble with them all week, so we left it. Perhaps we should keep him in custody while we check this out."

"I see, I didn't know. Okay. I'll take him into one of the interview rooms and get a statement from him. I'll see if I can make any sense of it all."

The two of them glanced round at Paul Denby and watched with horrified gasps as he drew out his gun and started to wave it around. "Now, do you believe me, or do I have to shoot someone first?"

The children watched the drama unfolding on the screen. The Desk Officer must have pressed an alarm as almost immediately two other burly Policemen rushed out of the side door that connected the reception area to the Police Station. They quickly took the gun from Paul and handcuffed his hands behind his back. They read him his rights and pushed him through the door.

"Phew," Ally said.

"Awesome," both Archie and Zonah said in unison.

Signet moved over to the mirror. "Fun's over now, so I'll turn it off."

"No, hang on a minute," Archie begged. "I just want to watch the small man."

The children saw him raising his eyes to heaven. "Well, whatever's next? I knew it was dangerous going into hospitals these days. You come out with more diseases than you went in for in the first place, but now it's even more dangerous to come into a Police Station with mad people raving about wizards, unicorns, temples and alien planets and then waving guns at people." He flounced off, flinging a last remark over his shoulder as he went out of the door. "I shall certainly think twice about coming down here again, thank you very much."

Zonah started to whine and held her stomach as she fell on the floor and stuffed her coat into her mouth. Archie and Ally, completely undone, followed her, rolling about laughing helplessly.

Signet switched off the screen and waited patiently for them to stop laughing. When he was sure that the giggling had stopped and the last eye had been wiped he said, "We've got a few loose ends to tie up now. I want you three to go to the Police Station and hand in the Faberge eggs. Say that you went to the Marina to go to the cinema but you found this carrier bag and thought you had better hand it in to the Police as you thought the contents were valuable."

The children looked at each other. Archie was thinking that his sister and Zonah appeared dishevelled, and Signet, with his usual perception, observed the look on his face. He pointed his ring at the girls and uttered the words, "Shamooska elvit venit."

Ally looked down at her shorts and t-shirt in amazement as all the mud stains, blood and dirty marks disappeared in an instant. She glanced at Zonah who was looking just as amazed as she was and then they both laughed delightedly.

"I'll TAM you over to the Police Station, then there are things

I must do urgently. I will have to block the two entrances into the sewers to protect the temple. When the theft from the bank is discovered, there are going to be all sorts of people clomping around down there.

"How will you do that?" Archie asked.

"I'll put in an invisible wall which will act like a shield. No-one will be able to get through it."

"Is that magic or Altairian technology?"

"Well, in times gone by I would have used magic, but everyone has to move with the times—even an old wizard like me." Signet smiled. "So I'm going to use the latest Altairian High-Tec."

"Can we watch?"

"No, there's nothing to see. It's invisible. You would only be prevented from going through it and there isn't time for you to try it out. Maybe later, mmm, Julian's disappeared, I'll have to find him and escort him back to Altair."

"Who's Julian?" Ally asked.

"He's the Altairian who Vastator tricked into helping him."

"What will happen to him?"

"Mmm, I don't know yet, but I expect he'll be punished."

"But that's not fair. Vastator deceived him. It wasn't his fault."

"Hmm, yes, well everything will be taken into consideration, so the Altairians won't be too harsh on him. I'll TAM you to the Police Station, now. You know what to say and you can all act surprised when they discover that they really are Faberge eggs and are worth a fortune. I'll contact you when all the fuss has died down. Good luck and thank you for all your help. I'll see you soon."

With that, Signet pressed a button on Archie's TAM and the children found themselves outside the Police Station.

Ally said to the others, "I think it would be best if Zonah speaks, as she's the best actress. She was brilliant when she played Lady Macbeth in the school play and I'd probably stutter."

Archie nodded in agreement. They were all a little nervous as the Police Station was a scary place, but the three of them took a deep breath and walked in. Luckily, there was no one at the reception desk and the same Desk Officer from the mirror screen came towards them smiling. It was the same one who had interviewed Paul Denby. Archie breathed a sigh of relief as this meant, with any luck, they might be quick. Ally also recognised the Desk Officer and uncrossed her fingers on her left hand although she still kept her right hand fingers crossed, just in case.

Zonah seemed to be perfectly at ease and smiled innocently at the man,

"We've come to hand this in. We found them in a carrier bag at the Marina Cinema. I was going to keep one and add it to my rock and stone collection and Ally was going to give the other one to her mother to put in her display cabinet. We thought that day-tripper had bought them on one of the stalls around the pier. But when we showed the eggs to Archie, he thought they might be valuable."

Archie joined in. "We've just done the Russian Revolution in history at school and I remember seeing pictures of Faberge eggs one of the books. They look a bit like the pictures so I told my sister and her friend, and we've come to hand them in."

The Desk Officer carefully took out one of the heavy bejewelled eggs and stood it on the counter. The other Desk Officer came forward and gasped. The egg glistened and sparkled.

Ally plucked up courage to say, "We can leave our names and addresses and if no-one claims them, then you can contact us and we can keep them."

Archie groaned inwardly, just what he did not want. It would be just like last time when all the journalists and photographers had descended upon them.

Zonah smiled at him, almost as if she knew what he was thinking and whispered, "It'll be okay."

There was a lot of scurrying about behind the Reception. Various Police Officers came to stare at the Faberge eggs, which had been moved to a central desk. The children heard snatches of sentences, "... telephoned the bank manager Mr Morgan, who confirms that…. Checking the bank now for signs of the robbery…. They may be useful witnesses…"

One of the Police Sergeants opened the door into the Police Station and motioned for the children to follow him and he ushered them into a room. The Police Officer told them to telephone their parents, who were at first shocked to learn that their children were at the Police Station, and then astounded to hear that they were the heroes of the day. The children were given cans of Coke, crisps, biscuits and asked question after question, and after many comings and goings, a Detective Officer came in. He told the children what they already knew: the Bank had been robbed and that they had indeed found the precious stolen Faberge eggs.

The children acted their part well and pretended to be amazed, with suitable murmurings of, "Sweet" and "Awesome." The Police officer told them that there could be a reward and they all whooped with excitement and high fived each other. Then arrangements were made to take them home in a police car and they left the Police Station amid smiles and congratulations from all the many policemen and women they met on the way out.

They dropped Zonah first, and with kisses and hugs the two girls promised to telephone each other in the morning.

As they left Zonah's house Archie cheekily asked, "Can you put the sirens on?" The two policemen assigned to escort the children home smiled indulgently. Archie was delighted with the exciting ride through the town, especially when they arrived home with blue lights flashing. As both Archie and Ally stumbled out of the car, Archie said, "What a ride"

He thought this was a perfect ending to a rather exciting day. Ally giggled and they both turned to meet their parents. They were both exhausted and the last thing they remembered was practically falling asleep over steaming cups of hot chocolate while policeman repeated the tale to their parents.

Chapter Thirty

The Ceremony

Ally climbed down the narrow stairway after Archie and Zonah and pulled the lever, which slid the stone back into place. Zonah gave a little squeal of fright as it suddenly became very dark and clutched at Archie's shoulders. Ally bumped into them both and, remembering how frightened she had been, said to Zonah, "Just close your eyes and we'll shuffle along. We'll tell you when we get to the lights."

Zonah felt comforted wedged between her two friends and she began to giggle as they moved down the steps like a caterpillar. As soon as Ally's eyes adjusted to the dark and she could see the faint glow from the Lumenite, she told her friend to open her eyes. Zonah cautiously peeked from under her eyelashes and when she realised it was lighter opened her eyes wide. The three friends walked side by side down the steps that had become more gradual and reached the door that opened into the Temple. Archie swung the door open, and once again they were struck by the beauty of the Oosha.

Zonah, who hadn't really had time to appreciate it the last time she was there, gasped in pleasure. "Wow! It really is beautiful the way the walls glow and the colours change blending from one to the other."

Signet stepped from behind a pillar. "Welcome, Archie, Ally and Zonah. You're a few minutes late,"

"Sorry Signet," Ally said, "but we took longer than we expected to get ready."

Signet looked at them all. Archie rolled his eyes expressively. "Girls! Signet, they can be as troublesome as boys."

Signet laughed out loud as he remembered how he used to say to Archie that he was a troublesome boy and that boys were all the same, *always in trouble*. Archie had come a long way since then and Signet was proud of him. He wondered how he would react today. Archie had seemed to have forgotten that Asphodel had said he would be rewarded, and Signet hadn't mentioned anything about it. They all thought they were just going on a visit to Uckbata, the Capital of Altair. Well, they were all in for a big surprise and Signet hoped it would be a pleasurable experience for them all.

Signet noticed that the children all looked smart. The girls had straightened their hair for the occasion and looked like black and white negatives of each other. Ally's hair hung in a shiny golden bell around her face and Zonah had curtains of shimmering chestnut hair framing her face. Signet noticed that Archie liked Zonah and smiled to himself as he realised that he was growing up.

The three children looked at Signet expectantly.

"Why are you smiling, Signet? Are we leaving soon?" Ally questioned.

"I'm just happy that I am able to take you to Altair. You are very lucky and it will be a wonderful experience. And in answer to your second question, we'll have to leave straight away, as the time slot is open till 9.00 are. Now we'll be back at 10.30 pm so what time are your parents expecting you back? We don't want to worry them."

"We've told them we are going on a school trip to Portsmouth to see the Mary Rose and we said we'd be home by about 11.00 pm. It was a bit difficult as both sets of parents wanted to pick us up at the school, but we told each of them that the other parents were picking us up and bringing us home."

Signet's matter of fact attitude reassured Zonah, who was feeling nervous.

Signet put his arms around Ally and nodded to Archie who did the same with Zonah. He hoped that no one had noticed him blushing as he did so. Signet pressed a few buttons on his TAM and said, "Well, here we go."

Archie clasped Zonah to him tightly and once again felt as if he was travelling through a kaleidoscope, with colours making patterns and streaking past in bursts. He felt a bump and swayed slightly, to steady himself and Zonah. He let her go and when he looked around he realised that he was on the same hilltop looking down at the city of Uckbata, the capital of Altair.

Zonah said in surprise, "Are we here already? I thought it would take much longer."

Archie noticed the smell of flowers that seemed to be much stronger than before.

The air seemed to glisten and sparkle and Signet and Ally appeared next to them. Ally looked down at the shimmering city below them, next to the sea lined with golden sands. The sun was shining, and there was a wind-borne fragrance of hundreds of plants like roses, jasmine, bluebells, lemon, grass but unlike any of them. The fragrant flowers grew in the meadow, but the flowers and vegetation were different to any they had ever seen. There was a faint chorus of trilling, shrieking and whirring.

The girls were spellbound and as they explored the meadow they each shouted, "You've got to see this. Come quickly before it moves."

Signet smiled as he watched them gambolling through the field until at last they came back to him, sated with beauty and novelty. Signet said, "Now that we're here, why don't you catch me up with all your news? I haven't seen you since you went off to the Police Station with the Faberge eggs. What happened?"

They all sat down on the Altairian grass and began to tell Signet their story, with great hilarity and excitement. Words spilled out and they interrupted each other adding to the tale.

Ally said, "It was awesome. The police took the carrier bag and then took statements from us. They treated us like we were royalty or celebrities. They brought us Coke and crisps and biscuits from their canteen and then they drove us home in a police car."

Archie broke in. "I asked if they would put on the police sirens and they did! So we arrived home with the sirens going and flashing lights. It was cool. All the neighbours came out to look and my Mum rushed out to meet us. She thought something terrible had happened."

Ally took over again. "Oh yes, and the next day the local newspapers wanted to interviews us and then all the national newspapers came round."

Zonah interjected with shining eyes, "But the best bit was that we were invited onto Breakfast television. It was so cool. We had to get up at five am and they sent a car for us. Then we went into makeup up and we were interviewed for about five minutes. All our friends watched us and they were really envious."

Archie looked at Signet and rolled his eyes meaningfully.

"So Archie, Did you go on Breakfast TV as well?" Signet asked.

"Yes," Archie sighed. "I didn't really want to but the man who owned the Faberge eggs gave us a reward of £5,000 each, and my Mum said I had to go as it would be disrespectful to him. When I got there I was glad, as I did kind of enjoy it. They made such a fuss over us and all the crew joked and laughed. In the end it was good fun," he admitted grudgingly.

"One thing we wanted to know was what happened to Julian, the Elf that Vastator tricked into helping him?"

"Ah yes, Julektar or Julian as he was known on Earth. The Ministry of Learning considered all the evidence and decided that his own shame was punishment enough. They decided to offer him a scholarship to become an officer in the Ministry, so he'll learn about how important their role is and help to make sure that nothing like this ever occurs again. He made a public speech to apologise to all the Altairians and it was so obvious that he was upset that I think all the Altairians' hearts went out to him and they have forgiven him.

"Poor Julian. He probably won't ever forgive himself though," Archie remarked.

While they had all been chatting they had gradually become aware of a few strange people walking down the road towards the capital. Ally had noticed that when they had finished telling Signet their story this had developed into a steady stream. "Wow, look at all the people. Why are they all going into the City?"

Archie twisted around towards the road and got up on to his knees. He started to point out to Ally and Zonah the name of all the strange creatures. As the pageant of the different species passed by Ally and Zonah gasped in astonishment.

"Where are they all going?" Ally asked.

She did not press Signet for an answer, as at that moment Zonah shouted out excitedly, "Oh look Ally, there are the Fairy children that Archie told us about."

They all stood and stared as a group of Fairies walking two by two, all carrying baskets, marched in two's across the meadow led by a bigger Fairy at the front and followed by another larger Fairy at the back. Two of the Fairies waved at Archie and the larger one shouted, "Hello, Archie, do you remember us? Melix and Xandria. We met you when you first came to Altair. We're going to the ceremony and we're going to throw flower petals when you walk the Shining path. We'll see you at the party later. We're going to do a special dance for you and we'll teach you the steps, if you like. Bye. See you later."

"What are they talking about? What is a Shining Path?" Archie asked.

Signet was fixed with three pairs of questioning eyes. He looked from one of them to another and then settled his gaze on Archie. "Archie, as you know the Council of Altair have decided make you a Citizen of Altair. This is a great honour and it has never been given to anyone as young as you. The ceremony takes place in the Town Square. All the acolytes who have passed their rites of passage successfully walk up to the Town Hall on the Shining Path, which is specially constructed for the occasion, and the four Shining Beings will confer you with Citizenship of Altair. This gives you the freedom of the City so you will be able to enter any of the Ministries, the University, the Libraries and the Technology Centres. You pass through an archway and your DNA profile is then entered into the system which is recognised everywhere."

"Cool,"

Signet looked at him and smiled. He did not think he realised the full implication of the gift that was about to be given to him. It would mean that he would be able to succeed in any field he chose. Archie would achieve wealth and celebrity beyond his wildest dreams, backed by the advanced technology of Altair.

Archie realised that Signet was looking at him strangely. "Does this mean that I can introduce new ideas from Altair to Earth?"

Signet replied, "The Altairians will not give you unlimited powers to import their advanced technology to Earth; otherwise Altair's existence could be discovered. They think that Earth is not evolved enough to handle this information, but they will help you to *develop* new ideas on Earth, which they consider to be helpful to its development."

"Wow, I can be an entrepreneur like Richard Branson or an inventor like Isambard Kingdom Brunel."

Signet laughed and thought, of course, there were no flies on Archie and it wouldn't take him long to realise the advantages that came with the citizenship. Signet turned to the girls and said, "The Council have decided that you will be treated as Acolytes and will have the opportunity to become citizens of Altair in the future."

The two girls gulped back their surprise and gave each other a high five.

Signet did not give them any more time to think about the news and said briskly, "Come on, we'll go down to the City. Abe and Sol want to see you all before the ceremony."

They walked in silence joining the procession down the main road to the city, but it was not long before the girls were calling out to each other as they discovered more and more interesting new sights, smells and creatures.

"Look Signet, is that a bird?" Zonah questioned. They all turned and stared as an extraordinary creature came bustling down the road at a very fast pace, with a small replica straggling behind. It looked like an ostrich with a round body and long spindly legs, but the most striking feature was its neck, which was long and snakelike.

It stopped waiting for its child to catch up and turned to Zonah and said, "I'm not a bird, you silly goose. I'm Jocasta of the Shamenite tribe and this is my youngest son Amadou.

Archie could see that the girls were pressing their lips together in an effort to suppress their laughter and so he spoke to Jocasta to divert her attention from them. "Please to meet you, Jocasta, I'm Archie Dixon from the Human tribe of Terra."

Jocasta turned to Archie and as he looked at her face, he was amazed, for rather than the bird face and beak he had been expecting, she was beautiful. Her face was a cross between a cat's and a Bush baby, covered in long and luxurious blonde fur with dark markings.

She held out her arm and hand that had been hidden against her body and said in a cross voice, "Yes, I know that you're Archie Dixon. You are famous on Altair and I learnt your language so that I could converse with you. I was chosen to represent my tribe and bring my youngest son Amadou, to the party for the youngsters."

Archie shook her hand and said, "I'm pleased to meet you, Jocasta."

Although he smiled at her, he was thinking 'what a cross patch.' She reminded him of Clytemnestra, the Hollingdean

155

parrot, and he wondered if all bird-like creatures were cantankerous.

Meanwhile the girls had recovered and were making a fuss of Amadou. "Oh look, Zonah. Isn't he cute? Look at his fluffy hair. Aren't his eyes beautiful?"

Amadou was basking in the attention and twisted his neck round and round and peeped out at the girls from under his neck tying it in a knot, babbling away in a strange sounding language. Jocasta let out a shriek and shouted at her son. Although they did not understand the language, the children could tell from her manner that she was cross and that Amadou was getting a telling off. He was facing away from his mother rolled his beautiful eyes upwards and quickly unravelled his neck from the knot. Jocasta gave a stern command to her young son and the pair set off at a trot down the road, Amadou looking back at them, smiling and nodding his neck as he went.

As they moved out of earshot, Ally could no longer hold back and she exploded with laughter clutching her stomach.

Zonah took one look at her friend gasping out between giggles and said, "She looks like big bird on Sesame Street and she called you a silly goose." And she joined in and was soon doubled over with laughter. She managed to say, "Did you see the little baby's eyes when his mother told him off?"

Their laughter was infectious and Archie could see the funny side and soon joined in.

It wasn't until Signet spoke that the children calmed down and became serious. "The Shamenite mothers have to stop their children from tying their heads in knots. It can damage their necks and there have been cases where it has been impossible to untangle their necks without damaging them and they spend their adult lives disabled."

At last they reached the outskirts of Uckbata. Rounding a corner, Archie pointed out "The Schlock Shop" to Ally and Zonah. Abe and Soli were standing outside waiting to welcome them and they both hugged and kissed the children on the cheek. The girls did not mind at all but Archie was always embarrassed by any outward show of affection. He was relieved that no one noticed his discomfiture as the two Mizakeen ushered them into the shop. Ally and Zonah were enthralled at the rows and rows of different garments on rails and in display cabinets all around the shop and they spent a happy time exclaiming over the variety of garments displayed. When they had finished exploring, Signet called them over to the front of the shop and told them it was time to go. They followed Signet as he led them towards the Main Square, calling out "goodbye" and "see you later" to Abe and Soli.

As they drew close, they could hear a loud rumble of voices in the background. It was occasionally pierced with individual sounds like a shout, a shriek, a laugh or a baby's cry. The children gasped in surprise as they turned a corner into the square and they saw the crowds. The large Town Hall was decorated with decks of flowers and ribbons, and there were banners flying in the breeze from all the lampposts and the balconies of the surrounding buildings. Their eyes immediately went to the centre of the square where there was a shining beam of light leading to the steps of the Town Hall.

Then everything seemed to happen quickly. Signet ushered the children to some seats where there were others waiting. With a fanfare of some musical instrument, the Shining Beings appeared at the top of the Town Hall steps accompanied by Asphodel and Aloric.

Ally nudged Zonah. "Look, Zonah, there's Aloric."

Zonah let out a sigh of relief. "He's alive. I know Signet told us he'd be okay, but I didn't absolutely believe him."

Signet heard and smiled to himself. He knew the children wouldn't quite believe Aloric was alive until they had seen him with their own eyes. 'Why should they?' He asked himself. The last time they had seen him he was lying dead on the floor of the Temple with his lifeblood pumping out of him.

More people came out of the great doors of the Town Hall and stood beside the Elders. Archie recognised some of them, Greatorix the Elf, Shasika the Fairy, Doctor Beshley the Bean Tighe, Souhei the Kitsune, Doctor Kiddush the Tokolyush, Yin Zheng the Fenghuang and Doctor Hokusain the Bokwus. He hardly had time to see if he recognised anyone else, for with another fanfare, a name was announced and amid cheers and showers of flower petals the Seraim, who was an Elf, stood on the Shining Path. To the children's amazement he seemed to float along the path as he was pelted with cascades of flower petals, accompanied by even louder cheers.

While the Divas were shaking the Elf's hand, Archie whispered to Signet, "What is the Shining Path? How does it work?"

"It's an outdated technology now, magnetic levitation."

Archie nodded. "Ah yes, Fingal told me about it. What does it feel like to travel on it?"

Signet laughed. "You're about to find out. It's your turn now," he said just as Archie's name was announced.

"Archie Dixon, from the human tribe of Terra."

"There you go Archie."

He stepped on the platform and held on to the transparent handrails and it began to glide smoothly along the path. He was so interested in the magnetic levitation that he didn't have time to feel nervous or embarrassed as everyone cheered him and threw flower petals at him. He heard Ally and Zonah chanting his name, and he looked round at them and grinned. Gradually the Altairians nearby joined in and his name spread from person to person until the whole crowd took up the cry until his name was being shouted, echoing round the square. It sounded just like a crowd at a football match except they were calling his name. Archie walked up the steps and shook hands with each of the Shining Beings and then all the other officials standing in a line.

He was bombarded with "Thanks" and "Well done," and when he reached Doctor Beshley, she flung her arms around him and kissed him, thanking him over and over again. For once Archie did not mind being kissed because it was a beautiful woman.

Archie stood at the side with the other Seraim and soon it was the girls turn to walk the Shining Path to be accepted as acolytes. When they had walked down the line and shaken hands with everyone on the Town Hall podium, they joined Archie.

Asphodel stepped forward to say a few closing words and the children watched as her words appeared on a wide screen nearby translated into English. Then she turned to the children and beckoned to them. As they reached her side, the crowd went mad, shouting and cheering and eventually she held her hand up for the noise to subside.

"I don't have to tell you all that we are delighted to welcome our very special guests from Terra: Archie, Ally and Zonah. Nor do I have to tell you that we owe our very survival to them. This is why the Council of Altair have made the unusual decision to make Archie a Citizen of Altair and accept Ally and Zonah as acolytes. I'm sure you will all take them to your hearts as the Rulers and Council have done. As you know, today is a very special day and there is to be a party for all the youngsters of Altair on the beach later today. All Altairians with invitations are invited to celebrate with our guests. So enjoy!"

There was a tumultuous applause and cheering from the crowd as the Shining Beings, followed by Asphodel and Aloric and the other Altairians filed into the Town Hall. The children joined the procession of Altairians and found themselves in the grand entrance hall. They were guided towards the freestanding doorway that took a snapshot of their DNA as they passed through it.

The children were wondering what would happen next when Aloric trotted through the entrance to the Town Hall. Zonah saw him first. Although she had seen him in the distance at the ceremony, when she saw him up close, she was overcome with joy that he was alive. She could not help the tears welling up in her eyes. She ran up to him and flung her arms around his neck, burying her face in his mane. Ally seeing her friend so affected, rushed up to Aloric and both girls sobbed into his golden hair.

Archie took one look at his sister and Zonah and to his dismay felt tears welling up in his eyes. He coughed a couple of times and wiped the tears from his eyes quickly and hoped that no one had noticed.

"Hey, don't cry. I'm okay, and as you can see, I'm very much alive."

Signet had been speaking with Doctor Beshley in the entrance hall and witnessed the children's emotional reunion with Aloric. He walked over to the children. "Hello, Aloric. I've just been discussing the tour that you're making with these three around the city. Don't forget to visit the tannery as I know that Thorin wants to thank them personally for saving his son's life."

The two girls recovered and their faces were wreathed in smiles. Archie bucked up as soon as he saw the girls beaming. Again he was affected by their changing emotions and he felt his eyes crinkle at the corners and his mouth turn up.

Aloric grinned back at the children. "Come on then. We've got a lot to see before we go to the party."

Epilogue

The Party

Archie led the procession as they set off towards the beach. He was riding on Aloric and they made a magnificent spectacle. The white feathers in Aloric's headdress bobbed up and down and silver ribbons cascaded back, mixing with Aloric's white mane. Atalanta, who was Aloric's sister, was carrying Ally, and Zonah was on Lilliana, her friend. Signet had joined them and was riding on Theodurus. Each unicorn had small coronets over their horn with matching ribbons hanging from them, which floated backwards in the breeze in colourful profusion.

Archie glanced back at Signet and the girls and noticed that Zonah was frowning in concentration and clutching Lilliana's mane so tightly that her knuckles were white. He whispered to Aloric to pull back until they were next to Zonah.

"What's up?" he asked her.

"I've never ridden on a horse before let alone a Unicorn and I'm scared to death."

"Zonah, you're doing great. Just sit back in the saddle and hold the reins like this."

Aloric trotted next to Atalanta and to distract Zonah, Archie chatted to her about their whistle-stop tour of Uckbata.

"I liked the Ministry of Information best," Zonah replied animatedly.

"Oh wow, the holograms were great and I found out a lot about Cryptology."

They reached the beach and the four Unicorns trotted along the golden sand by the water's edge.

"Isn't this wonderful?" Ally said as she looked along the beach, which stretched as far as the eye could see. There was a gentle swishing sound as the water moved gently back and forward along the shore.

"It's beautiful," Zonah rejoined and Archie noticed that she didn't seem to be so tense and frightened. They all trotted along the sand in companionable silence.

Aloric could see that Zonah was more confident and he called out, "Anyone fancy a gallop?" And as he spurted forward into the shallow water he came alongside Lilliana and urged her to break into a gallop with him.

Zonah screamed, "Noooooo."

Archie shouted to her, "Just put your legs out straight in front of you, in the stirrups. It's easier to gallop than to trot."

Zonah quickly realised that galloping was easier than she had thought. As the Unicorns' hooves kicked up a spray through the water she shouted, "Whoa, this is fun."

Atalanta and Theodurus followed Aloric and Lilliana, and soon they were all galloping along the water's edge, the spray rainbowing behind them. Archie felt happy. He had his sister and Zonah galloping next to him. The ribbons from Atalanta's and Lilliana's coronets whipped in the wind, mixing with their golden manes. The white feathers from Aloric's elaborate headdress streamed back tickling his face.

He shouted to Zonah, "Well done!"

Ally shouted, "Go, Zonah go!"

Zonah yelled back, "It's great. Yeehaaa!"

They all shouted in unison, "Yeehaaaa!"

Aloric pulled up when he saw the picnic site. The children and Signet saw a colourful tent ahead of them set back from the water, trestle tables laid out in a line, and groups of tables and chairs complete with parasols. There seemed to be people scurrying about everywhere. Archie noticed that there seemed to be a stage opposite the trestle tables as if there were to be a band playing. Zonah noticed that the whole area seemed to be enclosed with a rope fence. Ally noticed that there were many Fairies, Goblins, Leprechauns, and other life forms that she could not put a name to, all milling around outside the roped off area.

There was a small tent next to the large one and Aloric ushered them in. The children slipped off the saddles and went in. Archie used the Portaloo, splashed his face with water, and ran his fingers through his hair. He was out of the tent in a few minutes. When Ally and Zonah finally appeared after brushing their hair, applying lip-gloss and mascara, they went to join Archie, who was watching all the food being laid out.

"I wondered what the food was going to be like, but Signet told me the Altairians decided to make this a Terran feast."

The children watched while mouth-watering dishes were set out on the table. Each dish looked more delicious than the last. All the food was labelled.

Ally said, "Wow, I don't know what I'm going to eat first. It all looks so wonderful."

Archie replied, "Well I do. I'm going to have beef and chicken, with lots of different salads and French bread with masses of butter. Then I'm going to have crispy fried duck I love that."

Zonah piped up "I'm going to have some Chinese food too. I love noodles and mushroom chow mien and crispy fried seaweed, but I'm going to make sure that I leave a little room Banoffee pie and profiteroles, 'cos they look yummy-scrummy."

Ally and Archie said in unison. "Mmmm yes,"

Signet walked over and joined the children. Ally asked him, "Why are there lots of people outside the ropes?" Her curiosity had been aroused.

"Well, the Altairians had to limit the number of people attending the feast so they have only issued tickets for twenty representatives and their children from each tribe."

"Oh I see," said Ally.

"Otherwise there would have been so many people attending that it would have been a crush and dangerous."

"So all the people outside are not allowed into the feast?"

"Yes, that's about it, but they've come just to get a glimpse of you three. I expect they've brought their own picnics and will wander off down the beach. They'll still be able to hear the music though."

"Oh, so that's what the stage is for," Archie commented." What sort of music will be played?"

"Ah, there are various groups from every tribe, so you'll get a chance to hear a good cross section of Altairian music."

"Cool."

Aloric trotted over and ushered the party over to a table near the stage. As soon as the children had taken their seats, the Gillyaids opened a part of the rope fence and people began to enter. Soon all the tables and chairs were occupied.

"Oh my god!"

Archie swung round as Zonah gasped and saw a dragon approaching them. As it came near, he heard Yin Zheng calling his name. He looked around confused, as he could not see the magnificent bird at first. Then he saw him perched on the back of the dragon

"Archie let me introduce my partner, Yang Rong of the Earth Dragons."

"Pleased to meet you Archie," Yang Rong said in a deep gravely voice. "And this must be your sister Ally and your friend Zonah; I'm happy to meet you all at last."

"The Earth Dragons are going to put on a special flying display later in your honour." Yin Zheng piped up.

"Yes, we thought it was the least we could do to say thank you to you three Terrakids."

Ally, Archie and Zonah all smiled at each other at being called Terrakids, and Archie stepped forward. "Thank you, we'll look forward to the display."

Asphodel climbed up the stairs to the stage and addressed the crowd. "I declare that this feast in honour of our guests from Terra can now begin. I hope you will all enjoy the food and the musical entertainment. Please be upstanding and welcome our guests Archie, Ally and Zonah."

There were tremendous cheers from the crowd and as Asphodel descended from the stage, a group of elves with strange musical instruments took her place. The party had begun. The children, who had begun to feel quite hungry at the sight of all the food, jumped up, took plates and returned to their table with them piled up. Waiters weaved back and forward between the tables offering drinks. Ally and Zonah chose an orange-coloured drink made from Altairian fruits, while Archie chose a bright green concoction.

The announcement came over the loudspeakers that there would be an Arial display by the dragons. There was a burst of clapping and whooping shouts, and then everyone was quiet, in complete silence. Ally and Zonah craned their heads, looking back and forward each way. Yin Zhong fluttered down on to their table and pointed his parrot beak, "Look this way; they're coming from the east."

The children saw black dots in the distance. As these came closer, they could see that there were about twelve dragons flying toward them in a shape like an arrow. They hovered above the crowd. Everyone clapped as the dragons formed a circle and each one twirled round and round like a Catherine wheel. Then they separated into two groups, and one by one, a dragon from each group peeled off and flew straight at each other. Everyone gasped as the pairs turned on their sides and passed each other with inches to spare. The dragons formed diamond shapes and star shapes in the sky breathing fire from their nostrils. The dragons' acrobatic and graceful dives, tumbles and stunts drew gasps from the crowds. For the finale, the dragons plunged headfirst towards the crowd in pairs levelling out at the last minute to fly only a few feet above the crowd. Everyone clapped and cheered.

"Wow, I could feel the heat from the dragons' bodies as they passed so close over me." Archie said.

"Yes, I know what you mean. Oh boy was I scared. I thought they would hit the ground." Ally remarked.

"What are they doing now?" Zonah said, "Look."

The children watched in astonishment as the dragons hovered in the air a few hundred metres away. One dragon descended slowly in front of Archie and sat with his legs folded under him. To Archie's surprise the dragon said, "Jump on my back, Archie." Archie hesitated and Yin Zhing urged him to climb on the dragon's back. Ally and Zonah felt the wind rush past them as the dragon flapped his wings and rose slowly in the air. He stopped just under the others, and one dragon peeled away from the others moving quickly across the sky writing with what seemed to be a fluorescent pen.

Ally and Zonah gasped and then laughed with delight as they read the message that lit up the whole sky.

"Thank you, Archie, Ally and Zonah."

The crowed clapped and cheered. The dragon with Archie on his back flew in a circle and then gently landed back in the picnic enclosure. He flew back to his friends, and the twelve dragons blew fire from their nostrils and bowed their heads. Then they flew swiftly away until they were just specks on the horizon.

Archie exclaimed, "Wow, that was awesome!"

Ally looked around for Yin Zheng to ask him how they had written the message in the sky but he had fluttered off, so she added it to the growing list of questions to ask Signet.

Signet had deliberately stayed in the background, letting the children do their own thing, observing them from the sidelines, throughout the party. He felt proud of them. They mixed in with all the other guests chatting and laughing. They mingled with Gillyaids, Elves, Fairies, Leprechauns, Mizakeen, Fenghuang's, Dragons, Bokwas, Bean Tighe's, Tokolyusts and Kitsunes. He saw Thorin, the owner of the tannery with his son Zegar, approach the children. He hugged them all in turn and Zegar stayed with the children for some time. The Shining Beings, Kiera, Imrir, Assa and Erda made a short appearance and talked to the children for a few minutes before leaving. They chatted with Gretorix the Elf, Sashika the fairy, Colonel Gurin the head of the Gillyaids, Professor Santha the Sylph, Dr Beshley, a Bean Tighe and Dr Hokusain, a Bokwus who resembled a Red Indian.

Signet saw the girls with the fairies. After they had performed their dance in honour of the guests; the Fairies were trying to teach the girls the steps. Both Ally and Zonah were falling about laughing at their own clumsy attempts to imitate the fairies. Eventually, they did pick up the steps and rhythm and were able to make a passable attempt of the dance, and the Fairies were delighted. He watched them dancing to the Altairian music with Soli and Lev, who kept changing shapes to amuse them.

Jocasta had found the children, or rather, Amadou found them. He seemed especially fond of Ally, and she started to teach him English. By the end of the evening he could say his name, that he was Altairian, count up to ten, and say, "I love you," which he kept repeating over and over again to Ally.

Signet looked at his watch and saw that it was time for them to return to Terra. He found Zonah with Aloric. They were both sitting down and she was leaning against his back, laughing at something he was telling her. Ally was sitting with Jocasta, and had Amadou curled up and asleep on her lap. Archie was talking animatedly to Doctor Beshley, Doctor Kiddush, and Doctor Hokusain. One by one he signed to the three that it was time to go. Reluctantly they joined him.

Ally handed Amadou over to Jocasta, and when he half woke up she told him she had to go home.

"Home," he repeated.

"But, I'll come back to see you. I love you."

"Come back, I love you," he repeated sleepily and fell back to sleep.

Zonah put her arms around Aloric's neck and hugged him

tightly. "Thank you for teaching me to ride and gallop. I hope we see you soon. Love you."

"I love you too and you will see us all soon."

Archie shook hands with the three Doctors, and Doctor Beshley gave him a quick hug.

"Come back and visit us before long."

"Oh, I've has such a fabulous time. When can we come back Signet?" Ally asked.

Signet felt three pairs of bright eyes fixed on him. "In next to no time," he said.

They waved goodbye to everyone, sadly. All the Altairians stood up to watch them go and put their arms in the air and started to wave them and move in time with the rhythm of a song they sung, which was beautiful, but was like nothing the children had ever heard. The children felt themselves falling into the kaleidoscope with the sound of the Altairians song ringing in their ears. The memory of that sight and song would stay with them forever.

The End

What Fingal Told Archie about Altair on the Way to the City of Uckbata

DESCRIPTION OF PLANET, CUSTOMS

AND

WAY OF LIFE

Altair is a planet in a galaxy so far away that Earth's Astronomers have not yet discovered it. It has one sun and two moons. Its atmosphere contains oxygen and it is similar to Earth in that it has land masses, rivers, seas and oceans.

Time

Time is different on Altair. The Altairian day is roughly the equivalent of two Earth days. Half of the Altairian day (one Earth day or twenty-four Earth hours) is fully lit by its Sun, a star named Elyos. However, for six Earth hours prior to the dawn of Elyos, the planet is bathed by the light of the morning moon, Kalyx. Immediately after the setting of Elyos, Altair is suffused by the light of the evening moon, Delyx. Thus, night on Altair comprises only twelve Earth hours, or a quarter of the Altairian day. The "morning" and "evening" moons counter balance one another around Altair such that they are never both visible at the same time. Therefore, the seas around Altairian land masses have four tides every Altairian day. The peoples of Altair observe a year of ten months each of approximately forty Altairian days.

As Altair's orbit around Elyos is circular, rather than elliptical, there is relatively little seasonal variation throughout the Altairian year, which comprises some 400 Altairian days, or about 800 Earth days. The polar areas of Altair have less temperature variation between night and day, whereas the equator has hotter days and cooler nights.

Peoples

There are at least three hundred distinct tribes living on Altair. Each tribe has its own separate culture and territory but there is little rivalry between them. Wars are unheard of because each tribe respects each other's territory, culture, and customs. Different tribes live in different lands on Altair and have their own dialects but they all speak Altairian, which is used as the universal language of communication.

However, one common factor is that all of these separate cultures all have a rite of passage called 'Serai' at the beginning of adulthood, which involves the aspiring adult's or neophyte's visit to one of four planets. The planet and the region of the planet chosen are traditionally distinct to each individual tribe. Terra (or Earth) is the planet most often chosen by over a third of all Altairian tribes. Each Altairian tribe has a close cultural affinity with the nation or land in the planet it visits. For example, the Leprechaun people visit Ireland, the Giannes visit Italy, the Nunnchi visit North America and the Domovel visit Russia etc. They have visited our planet over the ages becoming legends and have a place in the folklore of different cultures in our world. They are only perceived as magical and mythical by the peoples of the planets they have visited. To their fellow Altairians, there is nothing mythical or magical about them at all. In fact, they think the inhabitants of the planets they visit are rather quaint.

The Serai

The most important event in the life of any Altairian is the Serai, the rite of passage to adulthood. Serai is a combination of a pilgrimage, a year out, national service and study expedition. Those who are doing their Serai are called Seraim. Serai takes place on one of four different planets traditional to the Seraim's own tribe. The relationship between the particular tribe and their chosen planetary destination is traditional, and tribes have built up knowledge of that country such that they become the experts or authorities on that area.

For example, the Leprechauns know the Irish and the Irish know the Leprechauns. If a Leprechaun Seraim suddenly arrived in Fiji, they would be a little lost as they had been taught about Ireland, its language, people and folklore from their ancestor's pool of knowledge in preparation for their visit. In a way, it is rather like when towns are twinned. While on Serai, the Seraim are ambassadors for their tribe and planet, learning about another planet and its culture and bringing back information to their native Altair. Seraim complete a study whilst on their visit, which is submitted to the Altairian Ministry of Learning on their return.

The Altairian Ministry of Learning has three objectives. The first is to ensure that no technical knowledge brought back by the Seraim damages the ecology or stability of Altair. The second is to integrate acceptable new knowledge in to the Altairian experience and incorporate it into their knowledge bank. The third is that nothing from Altair is exported to the more primitive Serai worlds that would compromise their ignorance of Altair. When they have completed their Serai, the Seraim become Seraiyot, full citizens of Altair. They are allowed to vote and take part in the governance of their tribe and the whole planet.

Seraim visit one of four planets. Two of these planets are more advanced than Altair and here the Seraim can walk about freely and mix with the peoples of this planet because both peoples are fully aware of the feasibility of space travel. The other two planets are more primitive and know nothing yet about intergalactic travel or the existence of extra-terrestrial life.

Of these two, one is Earth, known by the Altairians as Terra, a name that they picked up on their visits to our planet. Until the primitive planets have evolved enough to be ready to learn about advanced technology and other life forms, there is a need for secrecy. To reveal such information before the planet's inhabitants were able to understand it, would seriously damage that planet's development. It is only in unusual or extreme circumstances that Seraim appear to the peoples of that planet, and then in a way that seems more mythical than real. Every Seraim is given a piece of Theolite, which is especially important when visiting the less-developed planets, to enable them to be "invisible" when necessary.

Not all of the tribes on Altair are inherently good. Youngsters from tribes that are known to be either mischievous or downright malevolent need to be carefully monitored by the Ministry of Learning. The Kitsune linked to Japan, the Goblins and Gremlins linked to Europe and the Fenghuang and Earth Dragons linked to China are examples of such peoples. They are forbidden to bring back and use any knowledge from Serai, which could be detrimental to the balance of Altair. The Altairian Ministry of learning strictly enforces this policy. The penalty for such behaviour is withdrawal of their Seraiyot status and all its attendant benefits. Such peoples are known as Aseraiyot, the ultimate in disgrace, shunned by the tribes and watched by the Ministry.

The Ministry also ensures that no Altairian technology is given to the two low-level technology planets used for Serai. It was thought that firstly, the Altairians did not have the right to interfere with the natural development of these unsophisticated worlds, and secondly it would give away the existence of Altair.

Key Altairian Minerals

Theolite

This is the most important ore mined in Altair. While some of its extraordinary properties were always known by Altairians, it was only really understood when an explorer from another world arrived on Altair. His planet had a small amount of the ore and he was looking for further sources, as Theolite was rare. In exchange for being given a small quantity of Theolite, the Alien stayed long enough to teach the Altairians about this mineral and its properties. That Alien's planet is now one of the "advanced" planets to which Altairians visit for Serai.

Theolite bearing rock is mined by the Dwarf tribe is and smelted into the metal Theolite. Theolite has the power to break down matter into photons and to reassemble them. It is telekinetic and when held by a person and correctly triggered, it can also telepathically read that person's mind.

Theolite is used in the TAM's (Transastromitter) for space travel. The TAM is set to the correct coordinates for the destination and the Theolite converts the person or matter being transported into photons and reassembles them on arrival at the desired destination. Theolite maps the quickest route across the universe using wormholes. Theolite is the major source of power used on Altair for domestic and industrial use as the Altairians do not use petrol, oil, or hydroelectric power. They do use solar power for domestic use.

Theolite can also create a force, which renders anything within that force field liable to suggestion. For example, the use of Theolite can suggest to everyone within its range that you are not there, effectively rendering you invisible. You are not actually invisible but everyone else within the force field believes that you are not present. Theolite also has the ability to be able to release sizable amounts of energy on demand. All of these properties are present in varying degrees in a lump of crude Theolite ore, but when this ore is treated to become a highly refined Theolite metal, all of these powers become concentrated, magnified and enhanced.

Before the Alien revealed the true powers of Theolite, the Altairians still carried out a form of Serai, where they visited and stayed with one of the other tribes on Altair. When the technology for inter galactic-travel was developed with the use of Theolite, the Altairians decided to travel to other planets in the universe and chose two that were primitive—One being the Earth—and two that were more advanced than they—One being the planet of the Alien explorer that gave them Theolite. The other planet being the planet Zima in the constellation of Rigel which gave the Altairians the new wonder material that Abe and Sol used to make Archie's shirt.

Tam's were developed and each Seraim is now given a TAM that has been preset to deliver the Seraim to their pre-chosen planet and country, after the necessary language and culture training has been given.

Some of the Elders and Immortals like Signet, who have gained the necessary knowledge and experience, have rings or pendants containing Theolite and are able to use these to travel through space, as well as using Theolite's other magical properties.

The skimming stone, which Signet gave to Archie, was a piece of rock containing untreated Theolite that Signet empowered with his ring.

Lumenite

Lumenite is another important ore found on Altair. It was discovered that when slightly heated, it gave off a great deal of light and it is used in every Altairian home, factory, municipal building and mine etc. Lumenite has another property: that of producing light in the dark or in twilight conditions. The Altairians have found this useful as it makes switches unnecessary, as the lights do not work in daylight. Yet another property of Lumenite is that it changes colour when heated to different temperatures. The Altairians have used this property in many ways, for example to make jewellery, paint, and decorations on pots and vases.

Government on Altair

Each of Altair's tribes has its own Tribal Council with either an elected or traditionally selected leader called the Donus. This Tribal Council is in charge of the day-to-day running of their culturally autonomous tribe. There is a central Grand Council made up of all of the 300 Donus. One of these is elected the Grand Ruler of Altair, and there is an inner council made up of the previous Rulers, known as the Elders.

Elections for the Grand Council and Tribal Councils are held every five Altairian years, and Tribal Councils elect representatives to the all Tribal Grand Council. Only the Seraiyot may vote. As Altair is a peaceable planet, there is usually no necessity for regular meetings of the Grand Council, and they only take place once or twice a year. If there is an urgent situation, the Inner Council will be called, and a meeting with the presiding Ruler will be held.

Food and Drink

Some Altairians do not eat meat but would be surprised to be called vegetarians, as their diet seems perfectly normal to them. There are many different vegetables and fruits that grow in the different regions of Altair. They are not forbidden to eat meat and for those Altairians that do eat meat, Wokbatt or Moratim are their favourite dish. Naturally, food and drink are brought back to Altair by Seraim from the various Serai countries that they visit on the four planets, and some members of each tribe will have developed a taste for them. As they are not produced on Altair, these foods have a rarity value and are treated as delicacies, rather like caviar or oysters.

Velvberry juice is a mild stimulant but an extremely delicious drink.

Celix is a tea-like infusion made from a local herb, which is both nourishing and calming.

Potoc is grown universally and is a pulp-like vegetable containing proteins and vitamins. Potoc is used in many different ways as fillings for pies, casseroles and a type of Potoc bread. Altairians also eat a type of soft Crystal, which has to be mined. Many variants of fungus are found, both wild and cultivated, and are treated like meat would be on Earth. Honey is produced and is used in many recipes to sweeten fruit.

The tribes all have their own recipes and traditional dishes. For example, the Fairies make Shruti, a speciality dish rather like Crème Brule. Another speciality is Moora, which are rather like pancakes and made by Katchinas, who collect eggs from the large Moratim birds who roam free on the plains in the northern territories.

Money

The monetary system used on Altair is based on credits. Goods and services are exchanged according to their value in credits. Everybody on Altair either produces goods or carries out a service which they can exchange for other goods or services of equal value in credits. , which, like the Ministry of Learning, is responsible to the Altairian Grand Council.

Transport

The Altairians use their TAM's to transport them wherever they want to go, so they have no need for any other form of transport. Before they discovered Theolite with its amazing properties, they had a system of travel called magnetic levitation. This was used many thousands of years ago and is now obsolete, apart from "The Shining Path." This is brought out every year in the main Square. All the acolytes ride on a platform using magnetic levitation to the Dias where the Shining Beings are waiting to award them citizenship of Altair.

Bibliography

A Complete guide to Fairies and magical Beings: Eason. Cassandra: Paitkus, 2001.

The Grail Legend. Yung, Emma and Von Franz, Marie Louise. Element, 1989.

Ley Lines, Sullivan, Brian, Piatkus, 2000.